RUAN'S CABIN GETAWAY
An Explicit Age Gap Romance
Book 1
in
Ruan's Getaway Series

Ruan Willow

This book is dedicated to those people in my life who are laced in my
heart
and my dearly loved
wonderful
amazing
stupendous
kickass
beautiful
awesome
spectacular
incredible
marvelous
fans.
You rock!

Prologue

I scan my text messages on my phone. There's Sebastian again. He's a guilty pleasure, no doubt. Our connection has only grown stronger and deeper these past ten months. He keeps pressing for us to meet, but I can't risk that. Plus, I just shouldn't. He's mature for his age, but still, he's just a fantasy. Leave it at that. But, oh damn, what a fantasy he is! I'm not a user.

Sebastian: How are you?

Me: Fine. Thanks. Yourself?

Sebastian: Good. Can we do a video call? Would love to show you what you did to me just now.

Me: We just did that

Sebastian: So. You did it again. You are my Goddess.

I roll my eyes. He had started calling me that. The first time I spit out my coffee, narrowly missing my laptop. I can't stop my grin, despite his cheesiness.

Me: Ok. Just give me a few. I'm in the middle of saving the latest changes to my book.

#

And that's how it went. For months and months, us edging our relationship over the airwaves, until today.

Sebastian: Can we please meet? I won't hurt you. I only want to love you.

Me: I can't.

Sebastian: You can

Me: Nope

Sebastian: How about I do a background check? Send it to you. You've seen my driver's license

I laugh. Even serial killers have driver's licenses.

Me: I'm not anal. You aren't a criminal.

Sebastian: Let's talk. Can I call you? No visual this time

Me: Okay. But we can't meet so stop asking.

My phone rings. I answer it, steeling my gut for a fight. It will be our first.

"Hello," I say with the full intention of hanging up in five minutes. Besides, I have a deadline to meet.

"Hi, my lovely Goddess, my sexy beautiful sexy-brained Goddess." His voice is thick and husky like he just woke up.

"It's not that I don't trust you, Sebastian. I just can't." There. I said it.

"But you are missing out on the part where I can pleasure you into so many orgasms, it will spawn so much writing material for you, not to mention relax you. You sound stressed."

His desire to please was never wasted on me. "I appreciate that." I sigh and run a hand through my loose hair, catching on several snarls my curls always tend to tangle into. I work my hand through them to free the strands, wincing when I pull too hard. "I have a deadline I need to meet and I'm getting close."

"See, if I were there, I could be eating you out so you could then focus. I could be massaging your feet while you write. I could be giving you cock anytime you want it."

Well, damn. That's beyond tempting. "No. I said no."

"Please. I know just what to do to you." The lust in his voice makes my clit twitch.

"Oh, you do, do you?" He's just too good to be true. So, he's not.

"I pay attention." His voice is full of tender determination. "Ruan, we could fulfill each other's fantasies. It would be epic."

It would be a drastic mistake. "I can't, Sebastian, I've told you why like a thousand times."

"I don't care about our age difference. I've told you that more than a thousand times." He clears his throat. "I'm in really good shape."

I laugh. Logic is not wasted on the young. "Oh, I've seen you love. I know."

"Then let me come fuck you senseless. It can be just that. Nothing more."

"I'm going to Colorado. I've rented a cabin." The second it's out of my mouth, I regret it.

"I'll come. It will be a fuck fest weekend. And that's all. I don't need more."

I scoff. That's a lie. Or maybe it is for me. But me letting him would be beyond delicious. A sexual treat the likes I've never enjoyed.

"I'm buying a ticket. I'll sleep on the porch. Like a dog." He pants. "Until you let me in, master."

I am silent for too long before I let a giggle slip at the image of his body strewn across the cement, his suitcase his pillow. "You would, wouldn't you?"

"Fuck yes I will." He lets out a slow whistle. "Ruan, let me love you. Or at least your body."

Chapter One
FINALLY IN PERSON

I adjust my black lace robe with shaking hands as it had slipped off my right shoulder exposing my skin. I tighten the little ribbon belt at my waist before taking a sip of red wine with still quivering hands. His glass is full and waiting on the granite island. Butterflies flourish in my tummy. I fantasize imagining his hand holding this very glass, leaving his fresh set of fingerprints with every sip, sitting on the stool next to me in this kitchen. He will be here for real, and very soon. My nerves and my excitement fight for the alpha spot in my brain.

It will all be okay. Screw that, it will be epic.

I clap my hands and squeal in anticipation. Finally, I get to look into his eyes in person. The book I've signed for him sits on the counter with a big red bow on it.

I rearrange the cheese and meat platter once more. Will he like the appetizers I have set out? Will he like me in person? My heart pounds.

I light the birch bark candles the cabin has provided, as I take in a whiff of the roses he sent ahead of his arrival. Pure red, their aroma is decadent and lovely, their petals beyond soft under my fingertips. He sure is considerate for a younger man. I scoff. Maybe that's an insult but it's accurate from the history of my pathetic love life. Being alone at my age is not how I pictured my life.

I take a glance around the cabin, the wood-clad walls, the images of wild animals adorning every wall, the puffy beige and red furniture, the slab of rustic wood over the mantle housing black metal bears, and spiky pine trees. And all these windows with stunning views. It's just perfect for a cozy fuck fest weekend. Colorado makes good cabins. Well, maybe it's the mountains.

I smile as I finger the soft roses once more. Sebastian spoils me already, and we haven't even officially met yet. Well not in person anyway. My sister's words ring in my ear telling me I'm insane for trusting a stranger to meet me privately. She just doesn't get us. Besides, Sebastian isn't a stranger. Facetime counts as meeting, at least sort of.

I hear a sound out front, and I quickly set down my wine glass and run for the front door. My heart pounds harder as I jog; my breasts bounce way too much so I giggle. I resist the urge to hold them to keep them from bouncing. I untie the ribbon belt and let my bare breasts out free as the robe falls open.

I fling the wooden door open and exclaim, "Sebastian! You're here!"

He holds a suitcase in one hand and a bottle of red wine in the other. He drops the suitcase. It topples to its side with a clunk, and the wine bottle starts to slip, so I dip down to catch it. He, of course, has his eyes glued to my jiggling bare boobs that won't sit still worth shit.

"Whew!" I exclaim as curling the bottle to my skin, the glass cool but not cold. "Almost had a casualty there. Would have been tragic!"

"Oh, fuck," he says. "You're already naked." His eyes are wide, and his mouth stays ajar. His boner is pushing out the crotch of his pants. "Ruan ... I'm speechless." His brown hair, so perfectly thick and framing his handsome face, flops down over his forehead.

I run my hand along his bulge and squeeze it. "Wow. You are ready, aren't you?" I lick my upper lip, bite my lower one, and flick up eyes up to meet his. My eyes twinkle at him.

"Whoa. Wow. I mean. Whoa. Damn. I mean. So, I've been ready for this for at least six months," he says, his brown eyes tasty as a warm chocolate bar. "So ready. Me and my cock have practiced four to five times a day for this, as I've shown you." He stares at me, mouth still agape. "I didn't expect you to be so sexually forward." He still doesn't move a muscle. He grins. "I don't know why. I should have expected it, I mean. But don't get me wrong, I'm ecstatic." He laughs. "I'm beyond thrilled. Want this!" He coughs in his hand. "I mean, I want you and me. Damn, I'm rambling like a fool." The hand he just coughed into flies through the flop of his hair over his forehead.

I giggle and cover my mouth with my fist, as I greedily take all of him in with my eyes. I shake my head. "You are delicious," I mutter. I never thought I'd ever use a dating service and yet here I am, having invited this ... younger man ... to join me on vacation ... after chatting for many months, though. I press my lips together. Fuck my sister. This is justified. And damn, he certainly looks amazing as fuck in person! It's so naughty of me to indulge in him. I giggle again. I push all thoughts of me being as old as his mom out of my head.

"Aw, you have no idea what that giggle of yours does to me." His face flushes, and his shoulders relax. His smile floods up to his eyes.

"Oh, I know. Remember? You've told me. And shown me." I smirk. "Many times. Bless Facetime to the moon and back a bazillion gazillion times." The last image of his bare cock in his hands, him stroking it for me, flits across my brain, and my clit twitches.

"Oh, yes, I know right. Sorry, seeing you in real life is making me a bit brainless." He gives me a slow come-hither-and-fuck-me look.

I expect to see drool, but he closes his mouth.

I take a step back. "Well, come in, come in. I have a glass of wine and appetizers waiting for you." I swing my arm toward the inside of the cabin while I smile, a smile that tells him I'm ready to fuck, too, I hope.

He almost trips over the threshold of the door, as he stumbles in because his eyes are focused on me. His mouth falls into an even wider grin as a sigh escapes his lips. After glancing around he exclaims, "This place is amazing."

"I know. It's just gorgeous." I turn forward, but glance back and giggle. "Might need your suitcase to come in too, though; I hear the bears here are kinda nosy and get into everything that's left out."

He gives me a silly grin and turns back around to grab his suitcase.

"Nice ass," I chime. I lift my robe to flash him my buttocks. "I'll show you mine if you show me yours." I lick my lower lip; I can't wait to rip those jeans off.

The suitcase falls with a clunk on the tile. "Fuck yes I will. Try and stop me." He fumbles with the button on his pants and finally frees it.

"Good. I'm waiting with bated breath."

"Damn. You are even better in person than in your pictures, or on Facetime ... they just don't do you justice." He runs a hand through his dark hair, his eyes flaring wide and bright.

"Real is always better, love," I say with a glance back and a wink. With a sigh of relief, I set the wine bottle he brought on the island next to the open one and pick up his wine glass, swiftly handing it to him. I turn to pull out the bar stool for him and pat the seat. "It's all those real person nuances that get us. One reason everyone is obsessed with video. But still, video isn't in person."

"Well, our calls didn't do you justice either."

His palm lands on my ass cheek and he gives a squeeze. He leans over to whisper in my ear, "This okay? I can't resist touching you now that we are a foot away from each other and not miles and miles. I've been dreaming of my hands on you for so long. Too long ... it's been pure torture." He purses his lips. "But. Seriously. That ass. Fuck."

"Well, since we are meeting here at this cabin for an all-out fuck-fest weekend, you touching my ass is pretty much allowed immediately." I give him intense bedroom eyes. No tender footing allowed. Going right for cock, sweetheart. "I already grabbed your cock ... so we are good."

"Mmmm, well then fuck," he says in a hearty voice laced with lust, as his other palm grasps my other butt cheek and he double squeezes my whole ass. "I like the tone you've set. I'm in."

"Mmmm," I moan as he caresses my ass, gives my right cheek a light slap with a saucy grin.

I giggle.

"I want to take my time with you though. Just a quick touch. I've been edging since yesterday. So, I'm pretty fucking hot for you." He adjusts his jeans over the big lump at his crotch.

I give him a seductive look followed by a smile. I can't wait for him to jackhammer my pussy. "I can't wait to peel down those jeans."

He chuckles. "Oh, you have no idea how much I've wanted that." He scoffs. "My dick can't get any harder."

We both relax against the backs of our barstools, and I watch as a slow grin spreads across his face as he catches me gazing at his crotch. His eyes glow like I just gave him a winning lottery ticket.

"We are really here. Together," he says with a shake of his head. "I didn't think it would ever happen." He drapes his arm over the back of the stool, his thick masculine thighs set in a V as he hooks the heels of his shoes on the metal barstool wrung. "I mean, it's been months and months. I mean, we planned this weekend together. But ... I can't grasp the realness of this yet." He drops his head, then returns his gaze to meet mine with a smile.

It's a pussy wetting smile. Damn, he's cute in such a handsome way.

I giggle and lay my hand on his firm thigh. "And neither can I. I mean ... I never thought I'd meet someone this way, let alone a man younger than me." I bite my lip. Shit! I hope that doesn't offend him. His face twitches in amusement. I counter, "But, I'm very excited we've moved to this point though. It's a bit insane. Part of me feared you were a crazy person who intended to meet me and murder me. Chop me into bite-size pieces."

He almost spits out his wine but recovers and does a hard swallow of it under his laugh. "The only thing I'm murdering this weekend is that pussy."

I laugh and toss my mocha brown curls over my right shoulder; they topple deliciously grazing my bared skin. "Well, I'm looking forward to being sex drunk on your cock, cock-dead." I grin selfishly. "I can't wait for you to pound me out all over this cabin. Flatten all the juice out of me." I sigh as I look around. The tall windows flanking the fireplace showcase the majestic tree-covered mountains outside. The blue of the sky looms a parade background for the passing fluffy clouds. It looks like a dream. "Isn't this cabin gorgeous? I love the rustic feel of it." I lay my hand on the granite, my French manicured nails complimenting the white flecks in it. "The Colorado mountains are so beautiful."

"Yes. It's beautiful. But not half as beautiful as you are." He grasps my hand and squeezes it as our gazes meet. "I could say that every second, and it still wouldn't be enough."

My heart melts into hot mush. "Aww. You are sweet. Thank you." I take a sip of wine, sucking my upper lip into my mouth to prolong the flavor. I raise my eyes to find him staring intently at my lips like he wants to taste them.

He clears his throat and scans the cabin. "I'm not lying. We need to christen every room in this cabin with a round of fucking. Then go out and christen the pool and hot tub. Let's christen nature." He smirks, then his face relaxes into a sigh. "I brought a suit, but I don't dare use it."

Our eyes meet as our naughty smiles match. We sigh at the same time.

"Agreed. Though out in nature might be a bit chilly," I say. "But we will eat, fuck and fuck and fuck, relax, sleep, fuck again. On repeat. Swim and hot tub it naked. If we walk to hike, we could do a forest fuck. Weather dependent, of course."

"Ooh ... yeah. Fuck. Bless you. That's exactly what I intend to do, nail you on repeat, make you cum on repeat," he says touching my hand, stroking his finger along the top of my knuckles. "You are so soft." He grins at me with mischief in his gaze. "This is a gift for both of us. I'm not wasting a minute on anything but you."

Butterflies squirrel about my insides. "Same. We both need this getaway." No matter what the future holds, we both just need this. Geez, why did I have to be such a downer to go and think that? "Now. Let's relax with our wine. Have a few snacks. And then ... we can get onto the main course of our weekend."

He raises an eyebrow. "The fucking," he says with a massive grin and a nod.

"Yes, the fucking." I laugh and flick my eyelashes at him. "It will be epic."

"No doubt. I love looking at your hard nipples jiggling as you laugh. Just had to say that. They are such tight thick nuggets. I'm mesmerized by them."

"I can't wait for your mouth on them." I pick up a cheese slice and hold it up to his mouth. "Sustenance first."

"Your nips and pussy are all the sustenance I need." He takes the cheese from my hand by wiping his tongue along my fingers while keeping his eyes on mine. His lips pull the cheese into his mouth. "Mmm. Delicious." He takes a sip of wine and chews the cheese. "My turn."

He feeds me a cube of cheese, and I shove it to my cheek so I can suck his finger before he pulls it away, our eyes in constant contact.

My heart rate speeds up at the look of lust in his eyes. This is all so new, so scary, so hot, so sexy, so, scintillating. Yet ... so ... terrifying. "I'm not going to last long eating snacks with that look," I whisper.

"And by the way, you will get no writing done this weekend, not social media, no nothing work-related because we are acting it all out for real. Fucking and eating. That's the only work allowed."

I giggle like a little girl. "Well, I did bring my laptop, of course."

"Don't you dare. You are all mine this weekend." He shoots me a teasing warning look, laced with playfulness as his grin takes over his gorgeous face.

He slips off the barstool and pushes his body between my knees, spreading my thighs open big and wide, lodging the generous lump of his boner against the edge of the stool.

My heartbeat pounds even in my lips. My breathing rages. My mind spins.

"Yes," I murmur. "I'm all yours."

My hands meander to grab his ass cheeks. I drag my fingernails up to his neck while holding his lust-filled gaze with mine. My heart might burst right out of me.

"I want to fuck you," he says. "Now." His eyes are urgent, commanding, wanton, determined.

I smile while holding his gaze. "You just made my clit twitch."

"Mmmmm. Fuckkkkk yes," he says, as his hands dive into my curls, cradling my head, he suctions his open mouth to mine, his tongue riding into my mouth immediately, urgently, aggressively.

I almost slide off the stool, but he catches me. I wiggle on the barstool so my pussy nestles against his boner, thoughts of deadlines and crabby editors all fading into the background. Right now ... all my world is him.

He lets out a groan as we kiss. "Finally, I can feel you," he murmurs. "I've dreamt of touching you every day for months and months." He drags his index finger across my cheek. "Your skin is unbelievably soft. So ... wow ... like none other I've felt."

I tip my head to the side. "It is very nice to be touching you too. Coconut oil is my secret, hemp seed oil too. Every day. I use all the natural oils instead of the chemically filled lotions." I sigh as my phone vibrates on the counter. "So many video chats float through my head, of times I wanted to caress you after we played. Touch you just like this."

"Same," he murmurs against the skin of my neck as he trails kisses down to the base of my throat. "Oh, my fucking fuck fuck. Ru, you make me dizzy with want."

Our mouths crash together as our bodies collide into a tangle of our grasping limbs. Our hands roam and grab flesh as moans escape from our mouths.

Euphoria is within grasp, and I hunger for it.

"Mmmm. So hungry for you," he murmurs into my mouth. "I want to kiss you all over. Every inch."

My tongue slides into his mouth and caresses his as he strokes back, I grind my pelvis against his hard as fuck hard-on. My hand slides down his shaft and he moans out. My breathing ramps up to panting as I grip his shoulders, digging my fingernails into his firm flesh.

"Oh fuck. I'm going to fuck you into a sex coma," he whispers before biting my upper ear and nibbles down to my earlobe. He sucks my lobe for several seconds before traveling with kisses down my neck.

I shiver with delight, as I lean my head back and arch, forcing my breasts into his face as he travels down the mound of my left breast with his mouth, the script of our past sexting repeating in my mind's ear. Oh, all the fantasies we discussed bulge ripe as his cockhead. He suckles my hard nipple, as my hands delve into his hair. I massage his scalp, as he lets my nipple slip out of his mouth with a *pop*.

I gasp then giggle.

He devours my nipple again with a wide-open mouth, and I squirm against his suck, gyrating and moaning.

Words fail when mouth is on tit. I need to write that one down and use it in a story. I stifle my chuckle, as he mouth manhandles my peaked nipple with the delicious aggressiveness of a man, not that I've ever been with a woman. But still, oh, the deep expressed drive of a horny man. It's just unmatched in intensity. Holy fuck me now. Deliciously, I ache for his rough strong hands all over me as he mauls my torso, presses my waist and hips, grips my thighs hard.

My breathing turns to gasps. "Fuck, I want you," I murmur, as his fingers press into the soft flesh of my ass cheeks.

His arm secures my back, as I arch further allowing his full access to mouth mount each of my tits in turn. He bounces back and forth between them, his hand cupping as he lightly gnaws and suckles, pinches, and pulls.

"I love your nipples so much," he whispers before his mouth devours my left one again. "I'd always stare at your pictures on my phone, as I stroked my cock."

"Mmmmm. Don't stop, Sebastian. It feels amazing." I'm so relieved at the level of desire he's showing me. Passion is truly ageless. I smile as all my worries die.

He lets me tip back and my back slams into the backrest of the barstool which opens up access for him to get my pussy. He doesn't miss a beat.

I moan, as his hand tickles my lower lips, my wetness spilling to his fingers. He slides two in to finger me. "So very very wet," he mutters, his mouth sloppy with saliva.

"Mmm-hmmm," I whisper. "Very wet. Because of you."

He fingerfucks me fast, keeping his palm open to slap my clit, and I moan out. The skin slaps and the slosh of my increasingly wet pussy sound lush and sensual in the silence of the room. Those silent cabin skin-smacking sounds are scrumptious as honey. That's a hot name for a story, those cabin sounds. Maybe it will be our story if he lets me write it.

He straightens and reaches for his wine glass. After dipping his fingers into the wine, he drizzles it over my breasts then hands it to me with a smile. "More?" he grins. "I want you buzzed. Loosened up."

"Oh, I'm loosened up alright." I take a sip, my smile growing behind the wine glass as he quickly licks all the drips that dove down my breasts, sliding to my nipples then down my underboob.

He slurps at my right underboob than my left. He reaches up again to dip his fingers in and this time he smears the wine all across my pussy, purposely lingering over my clit, making me moan.

"Mmmm. Told ya, I'm a clit junkie." I thrash my head side to side writhing against his bold touch, which is making me even riper to be ridden.

He chuckles against my pussy lips, his hot breath a sensual bath, the hum of his hearty masculine laugh deliciously reminiscent of my vibrator. "Same." I want to eat that twinkle in his eyes, or at least suck on it.

I set the wine on the countertop as he lowers himself down my body, his mouth open, tongue slightly sticking out as he keeps constant eye contact with me. The first swipe of his tongue along my clit causes me to call out, "Oh fuck, yes." The rush of blood through my pussy is raging it to throb, my vaginal walls flare at the opening as he licks all over my labia lips and clitoris. I want that cock of his in me now.

"Oh, fuck, that feels amazing," I say as my head falls back as his promise of ecstasy unfolds. I moan as he pushes his tongue into my pussy.

He rides my pussy with his tongue in a tongue fuck as I hold his head between my hands, my thighs closing in to squeeze his cheeks, euphoria edging itself over me.

"Come for me baby, come for me, I want to taste your cum on my tongue." He wiggles his tongue back and forth across my clit for several minutes as I ride up the climb of my climax, then pulls all my lower bits of his into his mouth as I yell out a loud groan.

"Yes, oh fuck yes," I murmur as I near the edge of my orgasm, I fall silent overwhelmed by pleasure sensations.

He stands suddenly and scoops me up, carrying me like a baby to the puffy soft brown and maroon couch in the living room. The fire flickering from the gas fireplace dances across his skin as he lays me gingerly on the couch. The flames tickle the air above the fire, dancing in stabs as I nestle into the cushion.

I lean over, yearning to taste his pre-cum. I almost utter my request, but he crashes his mouth on my pussy lips so fast my breath catches, and I hold it for a few seconds before letting it out in a massive moan. I'm writhing on the couch as he eats me out, his hands mauling my ass cheeks and hips, as he shoves his face to my pink wetness. The eagerness, the lust, the passion is blatantly apparent in his mouthing of my pussy and blissfully the culmination of all of my fantasies of him to date.

"Mmmm," I moan as my sounds transform into nonsense words. "Izapa, Ijus, I ... Ffff ... uh."

His hot breath blasts my pussy lips as he murmurs, "Cum for me, cum for me my sweet sexy goddess of sex. I want to drink your squirt, your juice." His mouth suctions to my pussy even harder than before. "Mmmm fuck," he says when he pulls off me for a moment.

I grab at my breasts and pinch my nipples, tugging them before smoothing my hands down my tummy to end with grabs of my skin on my lower stomach, just above his bobbing head. Kneading myself in ecstasy, I mentally shift riding up the inevitable climb of my climax.

I twist my head back and forth as a shudder travels my body. I open my eyes just a slit as loss of control of my body looms imminent. The wind violently whips the tree limbs outside, as if a storm is approaching.

"Mmm," I moan. My eyelids flare open wide, then flutter as I'm raging closer to the peak of my orgasm and I scream.

His aggressive relentless wet mouth on me feels amazing. I fall silent, as I teeter over the edge and plummet. My legs draw up along the sides of his head, toes curling as my body jerks from the twitches my clitoris sends out across all of me. My body gyrates forward, at its own volition, my body a slave to my vagina. My stomach muscles clench causing my torso to curl and bounce. My tongue sticks out, as

I completely unravel, marveling at the point of how I have very little influence over my own body. Sounds I can't stop fly out of my mouth.

It's been way too long since a man had his mouth on me, and never before like Sebastian just did. As I float down from the massive orgasm, I let out a long slow sigh.

He slurps at my pussy, lapping his tongue along my opening. His sucking on my sensitive clit makes me jerk back, and he groans out his pleasure.

"You like to make me jerk, don't you?" I ask in a murmur.

He comes off my pussy. "Fuck yes I do." He licks his lips. "I'd never get tired of making your body jerk, shake, shudder. And by the way ... you are delicious, so sweet tasting."

"Yes, when I've tasted myself, I have always tasted sweet. Maybe because I eat so many fruits and vegetables. I like my cum after kiwi, and definitely after mango." I grin sheepishly, my expression is sleepy and sultry.

"Fuck, that's hot. You have mango yesterday? Keep eating whatever you're eating because ... damn that's good." He dips his finger into my pussy, and I watch as he brings his glistening finger slowly up to enter my mouth. "Should make you some mango salsa. Mmmm. Damn. I could eat this out of your pussy every damn day. You are so creamy wet. I love it." He swipes the finger through his mouth then slips it back into mine.

I keep eye contact with him as I suck his finger clean, swiping my tongue all around his skin. This is something none of my previous lovers would do. And I absolutely love it and I want more.

Chapter Two
PADDLE PASSION

He falls on me heavily, his mouth opens wide on mine, and we kiss. Our mouths seal over one another's, our tongues ride each other, our kiss its own sumptuous journey.

I suck his lower lip into my mouth and nibble a bit, as he moans. I run my hands down his sides, feeling the strength of his abdomen, his youthful fit body. My fingers roam his strong shoulders, drift down his chest muscles to pinch his nipples, his hard cock nestled against my tummy.

I grin unabashedly. When I was younger, I resented male strength because I lacked it. Perhaps I even feared it, but now I celebrate it because I accept it, love on it. Oh, how that strength can love on me ... that's pure lusciousness ... divine. Now I am confident in being female, gloriously so. I can't hate what I can't become. Truly, a gift of maturing.

I give him a happy satisfied smile. "You are next, by the way," I whisper, as he pulls himself off me.

"I want to take my time with you and you with me. Let's savor each other." The pure lust flaring in his eyes is such a huge turn-on.

I push him back on the couch with a devilish grin, yank his jeans down his thighs. As I push down the waistband of his underwear, his cock springs out, standing up mostly straight in the air as he fully leans back. "And savor I shall. But. First. Just a quick taste." I raise an eyebrow, as I take his cock shaft in my hand. "I love this smooth, packed ready cock." I trail my forefinger down a prominent vein on the underside. "Quick taste, real quick, I promise I won't make you spill cum, yet." I dance my fingers along his balls and cup them. "I want you to drive these nuts into me."

"Mmmm. I won't argue with that," he says with a sexy chuckle. "Ram my cock into your sweet pussy. And hell yes. Quick taste, yes please." He smirks with relish. "Ain't no chance I'm not coming though. On repeat this weekend." The crinkle around his eyes proving his jovial nature, his eagerness thoroughly delicious.

I open my mouth, circle his cockhead with the tip of my tongue, running my tongue tip along the underside of his swollen boner. I seal my mouth around and suck him as I stroke with my hand. His chest rises and falls quicker and quicker as I suck him. He lets out a satisfied groan.

"Mmmmm," I say, sucking him and popping off quick. "Shit. I'm not great at this. I have a gag reflex. Told ya."

"Oh, oh, no no no, it's so good, baby, fuck yes," he says. "Make that sound again, that feels amazing as you suck."

"Mmmmm," I hum louder.

His head has fallen back, his eyes slam shut. His hands reach for me, roughly grabs all my hair into a ponytail as I ride him with my wet warm tight mouth.

I sense him tense, and I come off his cock with a mouth *pop*.

I giggle, as he chuckles then lightly pushes me off him.

"Love that sound. Yeah, I don't want to cum yet." He sighs. "That was really close but felt beyond amazing. Better take a break, or I'll blow all over your face." He raises himself to sit upright on the couch, his delicious man buns naked on the couch.

I can't wait to see those buns of his walking naked around this cabin.

He fingers the base of his cock and shakes it. "I've dreamt of your mouth on me for months. Every day and night I dreamt of it." He runs his hand through his lush hair. "And my cock in you."

"Same." I sit next to him on the couch, plopping my hands on my thighs. "Well. Maybe we take a wine and cheese break, edge you a bit more. I know how you love that. And I have some sausage, jalapeno poppers, which are now probably cold, an olive tray, and a fruit platter." My stomach growls a tiny complaint. "I bought steaks to grill later."

He grins. "You need it. Yeah. I heard that little tummy growl." He chuckles poking at my belly. "Too sweet. Sounds good to me too. I'm really famished. Both for you and food." He stands to wiggle his pants back up carefully covering his hardon, an image I might just cherish forever along with that gleam in his eyes.

I stand up too, me naked and him now clothed, as he fastens his jeans. "Tight fit," he mutters while skillfully pulling the zipper up over his hardon. He smacks his cock with an open hand. "Look what you do to me." He lays his fingers alongside his engorged shaft pressing out his jeans.

"Well, fuck. I love that look. But if it is uncomfortable, just go naked then." I shrug, grab my robe and slip it on before we both stroll over to the kitchen island.

"I just might." He struts forward. "We can be nudists this weekend."

I eye his butt as he turns. "I'm gonna need to see that butt naked and soon."

He grins and gives an ass wiggle. "So, you like to cook, right?" he asks walking funny like a bowlegged cowboy.

"Yes, very much so." My eyes fall to his hard cock pressing out along his lower abdomen. Utterly transfixed, I can't look away.

He notices my line of gaze and a look of sheer giddy lust plays across his face. I return his naughty smile. He nods. "Soon."

"I'm getting a hankering for now, but I know how you love to edge, as do I." I grab his hand, and we swing hands as we walk as if we are long-time lovers walking down a forest path.

"You can edge the fuck out of me, however, you see fit. I'll stay hard usually for round two, or more, so if you slip up and make me come, no worries. But I do love edging though because I get so explosive." He pops a slice of sausage into his mouth.

"Yeah, that happens to me too but with being a woman, multiple orgasms, it's a given if keep going." I drop his hand and make a cheese and cracker sandwich. "I couldn't do it when I was younger. I was kind of a late bloomer with that. So now I kinda go and go with it."

"Yeah, women have it nice that way. But I just love making you come. The female body is a wonder."

I giggle because I have no argument there. "Well, that's true we do have it nice, but it's also much harder for women to come. It's always a given with men. And early on."

"By sheer anatomy, that's true. But I'll always enjoy giving you multiple, even if I'm done. But you first, always. I'm a gentleman. Plus, I have a mouth and two hands." He raises an eyebrow at me. "But I usually stay hard for round two and sometimes three. Four. Five."

"Wow!" Well, fuck. I do need him in my life, like so bad. I bite my lip and turn around to the fridge to pull out the olive tray. I pull up my robe to flash him a shot of my ass, complete with a backward butt twerk. "You cook much?"

He lets out a loud sigh. "Fuck, I love your ass. It's perfect." He lets out a whistle that tickles me deep in my pelvis. "I cook a little. My mom and grandma taught me a few things when I let them. I was a stubborn young dude." He drops and shakes his head. Looking me in the eyes, he says, "Well, Italian women are obsessed with their cooking, but boy, would they bicker about who had the best red sauce recipe. I was just there to eat, and it all tasted phenomenal to me."

I smile. "How nice though that you have memories of them teaching you."

"Yes. Such good memories because I got to eat it afterward. During. And the next day." He chuckles, as he shoves another hunk of sausage into his mouth, swipes his hands together getting cracker crumbs off. "The ways to my heart are my dick and my stomach. Though my brain fits in there somewhere, I'm just not sure how yet."

I chuckle loving his assessment of himself. "Good food is memorable, just like good sex, and a good conversation." The cold air seeps out of the fridge and gives me hard nipples and goosebumps. "Oh, don't let me forget. I bought edible chocolate body paint for the weekend, too, so we can paint and eat it off each other."

"You are a sexual genius, my love," he says as shoving a jalapeno popper into his mouth. "I love dating an erotica author."

My body stilling at his choice of words. "Want me to warm those up?" I ask with a tick of my head toward the microwave.

"Naw, they are delicious just like this. You make them?" He dabs at his full lips with a napkin.

"Yep, I did. I wore my gloves like a good girl. Once I didn't and then took out my contacts. Oh fuck, that was a big mistake. My eyes stung. And another time, I forgot and touched my pussy after chopping hot peppers. That was a big mistake too! Damn!"

He cracks up. "That's one hot pussy!"

I smirk, give him a dumb look, and stick out my tongue. "Funny," I say with a smile that otherwise really just hasn't left my face since our oral sex feast. "Sometimes I learn the hard way."

"Me too." He grabs a big blue cheese stuffed olive off the tray before I even set it down. "Speaking of hard ..." He runs his free hand over his swollen groin.

I slide onto my barstool and reach for my wine, my eyes flitting up and down from his boner to his eyes. I hold up my glass toward him. "Cheers to an impending weekend of amazing sex, good food and conversation, hardons, clit twitches, bed fucks, and snuggles." I giggle. "And maybe some new stuff neither of us has ever done. Remember our fantasy bucket list of things not done?"

"Do I? Of course, I do! Have it memorized." He grabs his wine glass, and we clink our glasses then drink, keeping eye contact as we sip. "You mentioned sex twice."

"Oh? Did I?" I give a flirty laugh. "I should have said it thirty times."

"Oh, yes did and no doubt. I love it." He taps the counter with his index finger.

"Good. So do I." I snag an Italian dressing-soaked olive off the tray and slip it into my mouth.

"So, you going to write the story of our weekend? I hope you do." Three more olives find their way into his mouth, and he chews heartily. Watching him enjoy food is almost an orgasmic experience.

I glance down at my wine glass, then nervously at him. "I was going to ask if you minded if I did."

"You have my enthusiastic permission to use me. Both all weekend and in a story." He smacks his hand on the granite. "I'm yours to use as you see fit."

"Yeah, I might just write one. Preserve our weekend in a novella. What an idea, huh?"

"A novel one!" he says with a laugh.

I roll my eyes with a guffaw.

"Oh, I want it. Definitely want you to write it. I would love to read it and know others are reading it getting hot, but knowing I was the one who got to do it all with you. Make it as autobiographical as you want." He rubs his hands together. "That's seriously hot as fuck to me."

I raise both eyebrows. "That's true. I seriously could write it. That is a pretty hot idea. I hadn't thought of it that way. I thought maybe you'd think of it as an invasion of privacy."

"Hello? Hell no. Tell them all about it. I'll get extra hard reading it, remembering this weekend. Then we need to read it out loud together. It'll be like a video of the weekend reading it. A replay."

I laugh. "Okay, if that's what you want. I'll tell the world."

"Oh, I want it very much."

I take a sip of wine and smile after I swallow it. "Okay. I'll do it." I suck my lower lip into my mouth. "I'll take notes as we take breaks. Keep it fresh and real and live." I cover my mouth with my hand. "Not that I think I could ever forget."

"Nice. Fuck, that's turning me on even more to think about." He swipes his hand over cock once more. "And that's the only work you get to do this weekend."

"Agreed." I bite into a popper, and it squishes spicy, creamy cheese and juice all over my tongue. After I chew, I say, "Mmmm. I love these things."

"They are awesome. I could eat the whole tray." He winks at me. "But I won't. I am a glutton, but I share." He pats his stomach. "All of them in this belly. All that you don't want. You first. I probably will eat you out of food this weekend."

I finish the popper and take one more. "The rest are actually yours. I've had my fill. I ate a few to taste test them earlier after I made them."

His eyes go big. "Oh, I'm in." He shovels them onto the little plate in front of him that's already covered in cheese, sausage, crackers, and olives. "A feast." He laughs like a little boy and points at his plate.

I grab a strawberry and slip it into my mouth as I nod. "Looks perfect. Eat up. Get some energy. I want to use the fuck out of you."

"You know just what to say," he declares, attacking his plate.

I slip off the barstool, still chewing the sweet strawberry. I walk toward the bathroom. "Bathroom," I answer the questioning look on his face. I wave a hand his way.

He nods.

I pause and face him. "I just got an idea from your video comment. I brought my tripod. Would you want a video of us fucking? We could each have a copy to keep."

He almost spits out his food. "Would I? Oh my God. You are an amazing dream come true. I'd love that." He grins, blue cheese dribbling down his chin. He swipes it away with a napkin. "I was hoping we could do a photoshoot and I can help you take some pics and keep copies of them of course. If you are okay with that, that is." He touches his chest and I wish it was my hand. "I love how comfortable you are with your body."

"Oh, wow. That sounds very erotic. Then we fuck. A photoshoot would make great foreplay. I like that idea a lot." My tits bounce as I do a little clapping with jumps which cause my breasts to slap against my abdomen. "Oh, yeah. This will be so fun!" I hurry off in a jog to the bathroom listening to his laughter belting out behind me.

"Might need a game of chase around the cabin too," he hollers after me. "You seem to have a lot of energy that should not be wasted."

My breath catches in my throat. "Fuck yes!" I yell. Oh, my gawd! I will wet myself down to my toes if he does that to me. Just need to get him to spank me, too, and I'll be a pile of cum mush. I'll break in this boy yet.

When I return to the kitchen, he has finished his plate. "Full?" I ask. He has eaten half the fruit plate too.

"Yes. I'm good." He runs a napkin along his mouth. "You full?"

"Yeah, I'm good. Cheese fills me up quick." I take a generous sip of wine.

"I'll chase you and treat you like the bad girl you are."

Geez. It's as if he read my mind. My clit twitches, as my eyes dart his way. "Oh? Chase me now?" My eyes stretch wide open.

"I know what you want. Remember, we've been chatting for months. I know your role play fantasies and I intend to fulfill them all." As he stands, he somehow looks larger.

I let out a sigh as my insides flutter. "Well, fuck me then."

"I won't hurt you ... much, but I'll definitely redden that bottom, then fuck you hard. Take you like a caveman."

Butterflies spin in my gut before my desire bottoms out into a frenzy of my excited nerves. "Damn," I say as my pussy lips flare. "You're going to make me come again just talking like that."

He nods on repeat as he says leaning toward me, "All weekend. All weekend fucking and dirty talk. You're going to be cum-wasted on endorphins. Gonna fuck you sleepy."

I raise my glass. "Making my pussy throb like crazy now." I take a sip. "And don't forget wine. I've got lots of wine and rum to make hot toddies. And we can order more if we need it. I checked. Deliveries will come here."

"Good. Now you'd better set that glass down because I'm going to chase you and take you as my own personal naughty cumslut."

I freeze as my eyes flare open.

He jerks and I flinch.

"Go," he commands with a lusty grin.

"Oh fuck!" My heart bursts into beating as if I'm already running.

He's young with long legs. I stand no chance at all, he will catch me in no time, but fuck I do want that. I swallow the last bit of wine swirling in my mouth, almost choking it back up as I get ready to dash off. I take a deep breath and run for the bedroom. My tits are flopping and my wet pussy lips slide across each other as I move my legs. I dash forward. I'm gasping, panting as I jog, but his height and size make him a beast, and he grabs me by the arm before I even reach the bedroom door.

His free hand swings and delivers wild slaps to my ass through my robe, as I squeal and scream out. He pulls me to the bed and forces me to lay on his lap.

I can't help but giggle as my pussy wets further.

Pulling up my robe to bare my ass, he lays spanks across one cheek then the other. I squirm on his lap, my pussy lips sliding across each other as I move, slickening me further as I wiggle.

I raise my ass up, presenting it to him, as he continues to slap. The slap sounds ring out taking up all the silence of the room except when he grunts, or I moan. The slaps send jolts through my pussy and clit, as my pelvis slams into his thighs.

His fingers of his non-spanking hand tickle into my pussy lips meeting my excessive wetness. Falling victim, overcome, my resolve comes undone, my climb to orgasm skyrockets as he simultaneously spanks my ass and fingers my pussy.

"Mmmm fuckkkkk," I moan. "I'm gonna ... " My whole body rolls into a shudder.

I moan out, as he manhandles me and works my clit with his fingers. I'm loving the contrast of both his sweet tender touches and his aggressive ones, blasting me at once into euphoria. My body jerks in a series of uncontrollable rigid twitches as I come hard, my torso curling around his thighs.

He stands, lifting me to my feet. "Bend over, you bitch whore. I'm going to fuck you from behind, slam into those red ass cheeks I just made." He pushes on my back to bend me over the edge of the bed. He lays a few more spanks across my cheeks causing me to recoil, and my pussy lips to flare, as I draw in a quick breath. Damn. He's gonna make me cum again.

He tickles his cockhead at my pussy lips and presses his boner in to penetrate me.

I groan. "Oh, fuck yes. Fuck me. Fuck me so hard." That first push-in of him into my vagina is pure ecstasy. Every masturbation session with him online floods my brain and not a one of them comes close to his cock entering me. I grab the comforter on the bed and squeeze. "Please," I beg. "Give me that cock and fuck the shit out of me," I grunt, then moan. "Please, Daddy, I need it."

He pounds a slap on my ass again as he pumps into me quickly, harshly, causing my pussy lips to squeeze at my clit just as I'm being slammed into the mattress. Bouncing on the bed, I rage into the edge of another climax.

I glance sideways, and the black paddle catches my eye. The paddle I bought for the weekend. Something I've never had done to me ever before yet yearn to try. I stare at it on the nightstand, hoping he'll notice.

He is too busy cock slamming my pussy, so he doesn't notice my glance, so I point at it, look back at him, and nod.

Slowing his pumping into me, he asks, "Are you sure?"

I nod. "Yes, Daddy," I whisper falling full force into the age role play.

He pulls his cock out of me and retrieves the paddle, his soaking wet cock swinging deliciously as he walks.

I watch him grasp the paddle's handle and squeeze my labia lips in response.

He returns to me, and I hold my breath, as he raises his hand. He brings the paddle gently to my ass cheeks and rubs my buttocks slowly back and forth. I push back against its cool flatness.

I close my eyes as the paddle leaves my skin. I hold my breath and want to scream all at once.

He slams the paddle on my ass. *Smack!*

The sound of it slapping my skin is almost as shocking as the sting it creates. He draws his hand up again and slams it down on my buttocks, forcing me to flinch in a deep recoil.

I whimper from the pain, which is much greater than I expected. "Oh, my gawd," I whisper.

"Fuck, this is making my cock harder." He grunts in this deep growl that makes my clit twitch. "Never thought it would."

He brings it down on my ass cheeks once more, as I yell out. He pauses. Then he slams it onto me again and again, as I pant and whimper. He gives a man growl, and my clit lurches as if it's been tugged.

I flinch each time and the force of the slap reverberates to my pussy. Fuck! Paddle on already spanked skin ... damn. This hurts, but it turns me on so much at the same time. I want it yet I don't. As a punishment, this must be naughty delicious. I gasp as tears threaten to spill out of my eyes as I'm wondering if he will smack my ass again.

He drops the paddle, and relief floods me as it hits carpet with a thud, and he pushes his cock back into me with a groan.

"Please, yes, fuck me," I moan out.

I melt into the bed, as he pumps fast and hard, slamming my clit.

I'm so high up on the edge of my climax as he growls again. He rams himself into me, I'm moaning and whimpering as he takes me. Every cell of me feels the primal nature of this and I'm about to tip over, my want maxed out at being chased, spanked, taken. I crash into convulsions, my body shaking against the bed as he pounds me even harder. I fall silent as I come. My vagina contracts in continuing aftershocks sending so many convulsions through my body that I can't even count them. It's like one long continuous orgasm. My pussy pulls at his cock with each contraction.

"Mmmm," he moans. "Oh fuck! Fuck that feels so good."

Wetness builds in my vagina.

I'm shaking as his hand caresses my back, my whole pussy throbbing. I try to speak but cannot.

"Whoa. Fuck yes, that was so hot," he says, as he continues to slow his pumping. But then he starts thrusting hard again. "I can't believe how I can do this. Oh shit. Oh fuck. I'm still hard." He speeds up his thrusting. "Fuck ... I just can't stop. I'm going to cum again."

My clit is throbbing, agonizingly so, it's so sensitive I cry out as he fucks me harder and faster from behind. Faster and harder than I ever remember being fucked in my whole life. I'm digging my fingernails into the comforter so much I fear I will make holes, rip the fabric to shreds like a she-wolf. My body is still shivering, jittery, my breathing finally slowing as I feel the darkness of passing out consuming me.

He mutters things I can't understand, as he pounds away so fast, my ass is jiggling like I'm being shaken hard. Another round of wetness fills me as he sighs. It's more a dream than real.

"Holy fuck," he mutters quietly. "Holy fuck. Holy fuck." He slows his pumping into me. "Oh, my God. I came so much." He falls silent for half a minute. I don't move a muscle.

I can't even will myself to move.

"Aw shit. Baby. Did I hurt you?" His voice is so filled with worry. "Fuck. I got so carried away. Are you okay?" He gingerly touches the tops of my ass and I flinch. "I've made you so red." He leans down and gently kisses my reddened cheeks as I squirm away from even that light of a touch.

"I'm okay," I whisper. "Thank you. I came so hard. Being taken makes me come so hard. Something about that aggression. That extreme uncontrollable lust. That gets me." I have never felt that vulnerable in my entire life, yet that wonderful.

He scoops me up and lays me on the bed. Crawling up to join me, concern plagues his eyes. He settles in next to me and lifts my chin so our eyes meet. "Tell me the truth. Did I go too far?" He smacks his forehead. "The power went to my head. I was a beast."

"No, it's okay. Really. I came so hard. Oh, my gawd. I've actually never been paddled before. It was so powerful, fuck."

"But are you okay?" His thumb strokes my cheek. "That's what I need to know." His eyes are filled with anger. "Damn. I just got way too into it. I lost control."

"I'm okay. Really I am." I smirk. "I don't know why but being taken like that turns me on. Dark fantasy I guess. But so do other things, so I don't need that all the time, but I'm really glad we did it together." I grin sheepishly, sleepily. "That was my first. Yup. I was a paddle virgin."

He lets out a sigh. "Well, me too. I mean, I've spanked a woman during sex with my hand, but never a paddle." He sighs as he rubs my cheek softly. "Oh, thank God you aren't mad at me. I was so afraid I went too far. I got pretty riled up. But that was so fucking hot." He runs a hand through his hair. "I don't think I've ever gotten that primal in sex before."

"Yeah, it was primal. Really primal. And yes, you did go ballistic." I let out a sigh as his expression falls into one of sheer terror. "My skin stings like a motherfucker, but that was hot as fuck. It was hot."

His face relaxes as he pulls me close and we snuggle, his cock still semi-hard pressed against me. "I want us to be each other's fantasies. Maybe ones we've never tried in real life, but we've always wanted. That okay with you? But we still have our rules."

I nod against his chest. "Yes, our rules." I cringe. Some wants don't mesh with reality at all. But this went okay for me. Better than okay. "I'm game if you are."

"Oh, definitely. I'm feeling sleepy after that big load and all that ... spanking." He chuckles. "Ass spanking. Might need you to spank me, Mommy, for raging on you so hard." He sighs and hugs me tight. "How about a nap, my pretty mama?"

"I'm in. We are in the right place for it. Let's get under the covers though." I scramble up readying to slip in.

We sneak under the covers, my skin still tender as the blankets fall on me.

"And you are sure I didn't hurt you too bad?"

"Don't worry, Sebastian. I'll be fine." What a sweet man.

"Okay, Ruan. But I think the paddle goes in the drawer for the rest of the day, or possibly for the rest of the weekend."

"I'm good. But yes, that makes sense to me. So. We can move on to other fantasies now."

"Yes. And now let's rest. Sleep good," he mutters, as he kisses my forehead.

"Sleep good." I'm so exhausted I crash immediately.

Chapter Three
MILF & STEPSON

The first thing I notice when I wake is my stinging ass. I grin and silently chuckle, as I gaze at him still asleep. The intensity of our fucking has my head spinning even after the nap. Amanda is right, young bucks fuck hard. Somehow it seems I've forgotten the thrusting power of men from my youth, or maybe I've just missed the passion of a very horny man hungry for me.

I slip out of the bed, slowly, painfully so, and grab my terry cloth robe off the hook in the bathroom. Walking out into the living room, the streams of afternoon sunlight bounce off the glittery white candles on the coffee table, glinting brilliantly off the shards of glass. The bowl of cinnamon-scented pinecones nestled next to them scents the air deliciously, as I breathe their wafting aroma deeply in.

This might be a mistake, but this weekend is just what I needed after breaking up with my ex a year and a half ago. We just didn't mesh anymore and try as hard as we could, we never could align. His love for all things quickie always left me desperately wanting for more.

I touch the cool glass of the window. I really thought this weekend would never work, but here we are doing it. The leaves on the trees in the backyard are all red and yellow already, catching the sunlight in the webs of their dying foliage. In this way, death is beautiful, or maybe it's more like sleep is beautiful. Sleeping trees in the peaceful slumber of fall to spring. The sun is so bright on the rain-filled leaves I can almost smell them.

His hand drops to my shoulder, and I jump and spin around. "Oh!" I exclaim. "You scared me."

"I woke and was missing my sex goddess angel next to me, so I came looking for her." He pulls me into a big bear hug.

"Just looking at this beautiful view. It's stunning out there."

"It's stunning in here." He snakes his hands into my robe and cups my right breast. "And in here." He nuzzles his face into the top of my head. "Let's sip some more wine by the fire, shall we? Before we grill?"

I nod feasting on his sexy naked body. "And before you feel the need to ask, I'm still fine. I'll recover just fine. It's just skin."

"I know, but ... I ... I need to check myself next time."

"No buts. Not that kind of butt." I giggle. "No apologies. Only sexy talk. Fucking. And fantasies fulfilled. Okay? And, plus, I asked for it. Remember that." I point my index finger at his face and shake it.

He nods. "Okay. I'll buy that." He grabs my hand and leads me to the kitchen. "You plan any dessert besides the chocolate body paint?" He scans the full countertop.

I chuckle at the hungry look in his eyes again. "Oh, yes. I have brownies and cheesecake, for whenever we want them. Remember I arrived two days before you. I've been cooking. Planning our meals."

"You're so amazing. I can't wait to taste more of your cooking. I love a woman who can cook. My cock and my stomach. You now own both of them."

I press my lips together to prevent a giant smile from erupting. I pat the barstool, and he takes a seat. Swiftly I grab the wine bottle and refill both our glasses. "Let me prep the rolls while you sip wine, then we can go to the couch. We can relax. Enjoy the fire and the view."

"Sounds perfect to me." He grabs the last piece of mango on the plate and pops it into his mouth. "Taking your lead. Fruit-flavored cum."

I grin, as he picks at the fruit plate, slipping grapes and pineapple chunks into his mouth swifter than it looks like he has time to chew one.

I giggle. "You surely will taste sweet now."

"Oh, I bet so," he says with a big grin. "You will have to let me know. I have a pineapple fetish for that reason." His hearty laugh fills the already cozy kitchen with warmth and brilliant sounds.

"You are a pleasure." My whole body smiles.

I smirk as he examines a strawberry before shoving it into his mouth.

I bite my lip with a chuckle, as I spray the pan with cooking spray, then lay out the frozen rolls evenly across the pan. "I think these need like three to four hours to rise and thaw, so it should be perfect timing." I cover the rolls with a sprayed sheet of kitchen wrap, wrapping it around the curled edges of the metal pan.

"What else are we having, miss chef?" He inserts a slice of kiwi into his mouth.

Who knew a man eating fruit could be so erotic? Fuck!

I swallow my lust and say, "Tomato, basil, and fresh mozzarella salad with marinated mushrooms and balsamic vinegar drizzle. Plus, smashed little baked potatoes laced with garlic and butter."

"Well, damn. That sounds amazing. I can't wait." His eyes flare big as he licks juice off his full upper lip. "You are going to spoil me so bad I'll never want to leave you. All this nakedness, sex, and good food. Better company."

We drift to the couch, wine glasses in hand. We cuddle up, each taking sips of wine in between touching each other in various places.

"I can't keep my hands off of you." His voice is so seductive I just want to push him back and slide down his swollen shaft.

"Same," I whisper, my desire for him somehow raging further.

"Okay. So, it's only early on day one and we have already christened the living room and the bedroom. Kudos to us. So ... how many rooms are left? I guess I haven't even taken the time to look around." He swivels his head to gaze about the cabin. "I've been just so focused on you."

"Oh, I'm not complaining one bit. Well, we've both been too busy eating and fucking and sucking to do so." I bite my lip as I gaze into his eyes, so brown and warm and kind. I want to know all the stories inside them. "There's another bedroom and an office. The office is an office and exercise room combined so lots of potential for crazy positions there. Then there is the little heated pool in the backyard and the hot tub too."

"Ah yes. That's all perfect. Pretty sure I could live here and be happy as a damn clam forever." He grins as he gently caresses my cheek. "With you of course. Only you." He gets a wild look in his eyes and purses his lips. "And. We also need to watch porn and fuck."

I giggle. "Ooooh. We have a lot of tasty plans. We might need another weekend."

A slow grin spreads across his face. "Oh, yeah. I would love that. I'm totally in."

"Me too," I say with downcast eyes. I follow the lines in the rug with my eyes. "No strings. We agreed. But we enjoy each other and whatever the future brings, it brings. It's just about us having sexy fun with each other." Could never marry him. I'd never live it down with family and friends.

He nods. "Yes. Agreed."

"Okay. Off that and back to sexual programming." I grin. "What's next oh sex guru?"

"I think you are the guru. You write it. But I'd be up for some naughty stepmom and stepson role-play or the pool or the hot tub or ... I bend you over the desk in the office ... we fuck by the fire ... we make our homemade porn."

I laugh as he rattles them all off. "Gee. You're not excited, are you?"

"Oh, fuck. I'm so excited." He points to the giant bulge in his pants. "I think I've told you a thousand times you are my ultimate fantasy. My ultimate woman. And now that I've tasted you, I don't think I can ever get enough, Mama."

"Mmmmm. I see that. Mama likes."

"Ah!" he exclaims overjoyed. "Then MILF and stepson it is! Oh, fuck yes!" He claps his hand on his thigh. "My sexual fantasy world coming to life. Right here, right now. And even better ... it's with you." He sits up straight. "How about you are messing around in the kitchen, and I come up behind you and pull your pants down. You can act however you want. Be shocked, slap me, you know, or hump me back with that amazing ass." He laughs. "Ladies choice on how it plays out. I just want my cock in you somehow way shape or form, Mommy."

"That's a given." I raise my eyebrow and give him a smirk.

"Okay. Let's finish our drinks and get to it. I'm horny as fuck for you." The lusty twinkle in his eyes stirs the butterflies in my gut.

"I'm pretty sure that look is making my pussy leak on this couch right now."

"Success." His hand goes right to my pussy, and he probes his fingers into me.

"Yep, fuck, you are crazy wet. Yummy." He jerks his head as he says it. My own little, not so little, Italian Stallion.

"How tall are you again?" I press my lips together. "I feel so short next to you."

"I'm six-one. And you are perfect."

He pulls his hand away from my pussy. "I'm going outside. You go make something in the kitchen and I'll walk in." We both stand, chug the rest of our wine. "I'm your stepson and my dad isn't home. I'm just home from college."

"I'm going to change for effect. So, give me a few minutes." I smile at him as he sets his glass on the island in the kitchen, he jumps with a little zing in his step, kicks out a leg.

I chuckle at his exuberance.

"Will do. I'll take in the scenery out front." He closes the door behind him with a saucy look back at me before he pulls it all the way shut.

I scurry to the bedroom and grab my little black dress from the closet. I giggle like a young girl as I slip it on, remaining bra-less and commando. I sneak my feet into some black heels like I'm just home from work. The dress fits snugly over my hips and ass, and chest as I smooth it down my body with my hands. I dash to the bathroom and add some powder to take the shine off my face. Ogling myself in the mirror, I adjust my dress to show maximum cleavage. I smile in the mirror as I bite my lower lip. I do a little jump and shimmy my shoulders when I land. This is gonna be steamy.

I walk as hurriedly as I can in my heels, my dress inching up a bit as I take bigger steps than I should. I want to get in place before he enters. In the kitchen, I grab a knife and bend over to look for the salad bowl, because I really need one for dinner. That's not the fake part. As I'm bent over, a hand slips inside my dress and cups my ass cheek.

I jump. "Oh, fuck. You scared me! I didn't hear you come in." I glance back at him, his arm shoved up my dress. "Um ..."

"Where's Dad?" he asks with a lusty smirk and a jerk of his head.

"He's ... at the store buying lumber for the bookshelf he's building me."

"I have lumber for you, Mommy." He slips his other hand up my dress so both hands are holding an ass cheek.

"Your hands are ... I mean, what are you doing, Sebastian?"

I straighten and try to turn around, but his hands slip out of my dress and grip my biceps, forcing me forward over the counter. My tits crush onto the cool surface as he presses my back down.

"What are you doing?" I fake my complaint in an appalled voice. "You can't do this. I'm your stepmom. Sebastian, no!" My pussy wets, and I grin suppressing a guffaw.

"Yeah. And I've seen you floating around the house in barely anything. Tempting me. Flaunting, teasing, egging me on. You turn me the fuck on, Mom. Dad doesn't have to know. We can just fuck. You know. Just. Get off. It's just sex." He slips my dress up to bare my ass. "Oh, I see someone has been naughty. My dad spank dat ass red?"

"Yes, he did. This morning." My tits press into the counter harder as he presses firmly on my back.

"Did he get off? Did you come pretty for Daddy?"

"No. I mean. I did. Yes. I smeared his cock good," I huff. "Not that it's any of your business."

"Good. Now you can smear mine." He rubs his hard cock along my ass crack. "I wanna give you a spanking, but I'll save that for next time, given your flaming red right now. I'm not sadistic."

"We can't do this. Your dad will never forgive us."

He laughs and runs a hand down my back, neck to the top of my ass crack. "I don't hear any refusals, only fear of getting caught." He pushes my dress further up the middle of my back. "I really wanna see those tits. I've seen those thick nips through sheer shirts but never have I seen those hard nipples in the flesh."

I pause and let him slide my dress up and over my head, tossing it behind him as he spins me around. My breasts swing and settle with the stopping of my movement.

"Fuck. Fuck me. Mom. You have the best tits ever. Damn, Mom." He cups my breasts, and I try to lean back as his open mouth lands on my right nipple.

"Wait. Really. We can't do this. Sebastian, we just can't do it. I … fuck, that feels amazing. But we need to stop."

"How about we just be mouth buddies?" he says before consuming my breast with his mouth. "Some oral fun."

I glance his way and snag his gaze.

He gives me a sexy grin. "I'll eat you out. You suck my cock. We call it done."

I tilt my head to the side, press my lips together. "Okay. So that's it then. And we don't tell you're your father. Ever. Our secret forever."

He grins at me salaciously, hooks his hands under my armpits, and lifts me to sit on the counter. "Now no pussy juice on the cutting board, Mom," he snickers, as he pulls the cutting board out from under my ass.

"Yes, sir."

"Call me 'Daddy,' Mom." He leans into me, a slight smile sneaking across his lips as he's lining his mouth up with my pussy, pushing my thighs back to open up me up wide for his tongue. His hot breath on my pussy a humid promise of wet licks, and massive orgasms.

I shudder in anticipation. I lean back and dip my head down toward my chin.

"Fuck. I've been watching you for the past three years parading around hot as absolute fuck. Now that I'm eighteen, I'm gonna take you, Mom."

I press slightly on his head, as I scoot back.

"Do you really want me to stop? I bet I'm way better than my dad is at this. Wanna find out?"

I droop my shoulders and stifle a grin. "Yes. Yes, I do, Daddy – son, sir ... I mean Daddy."

"That's better. Now get ready to squirt all over my face. I'm kickass at eating pussy." His mouth crashes on me, sucking the loose flesh of my clit right into his mouth.

"OMIGOD yes!" I gasp as his hands firmly grip my hips and he pushes his face smashed into my pussy. My hands fly to his hair, and I press my fingers into his scalp as I moan. "Oh, my gosh. Oh, my gosh." My heartbeat flutters in my throat as he devours my pussy, oh so hungry as fuck.

He wiggles his tongue back and forth across my erect clit, lapping his tongue along my slit before forcing his tongue into my vagina. He tongue fucks me for about a minute while wiggling his thumb flat against my clit. He situates his mouth directly over my clit. As he takes my flesh into his mouth, his fingers sink into my pussy.

I groan loudly, lean, drop my chin to my chest, and then tilt it back as I moan out and whimper.

He is mouthing me so aggressively, and he has me pinned to the counter, I try to scoot away, but I go nowhere.

It's so fucking intense I want to squirm away, yet I want to let him overwhelm me, take me. "Ohmifuckinggah ... fuck! So," I pant. "So, fucking intense ... "

He groans with his mouth full of me.

"I'm going to come ... I'm going to come. Oh, my gawd!" My climax peaks, my euphoria speckled with fear. Can tell, this is gonna be a big one ... and I topple over it, as he forces me to come. My limbs draw up to my body, and my body jerks repeatedly, as my vagina convulses as I come hard.

He slurps up my cum out of my pussy, moaning as he does, squeezing his fingers into the skin of my hips as he nods his head up and down so that his tongue follows in longer swipes.

I cringe when his tongue touches my clit. "Oh," I exclaim and jerk, as he presses his tongue against my sensitive clit, my arms stiffening, as I tip my head back.

"Mmmm. That good, baby?" he asks, as we finally make eye contact.

I sigh. "It's so sensitive, it almost hurts. Fuck."

"Means you came hard. I love it." He stands up and pulls me close for a kiss. "Dad ever make that happen for you like that?"

"Well, not so much. Not that strongly. He usually comes too fast."

"Well, he has a tongue, doesn't he?"

I giggle with a hearty clearing of my throat. "Not like yours apparently. The good tongue genes skipped him."

He grins, cupping my head in his hands as he kisses me deeply. Not a single worry occupies my brain right now. He is such an oasis for me.

I pull back and whisper, "That was exquisite. Amazing. Verging on divine. Thank you."

"My absolute pleasure. I love eating pussy. That's real me. Not role-play me." He grins.

I push him back slightly and slip off the counter and drop to my knees. I undo his pants and tug them down. Pulling on his underwear elastic makes his hard cock spring out in my face, just missing smacking me.

We both chuckle, as I grab for his still bouncing cock. "Think that fruit is working yet?"

I grin up at him as he's clearly helping it swing more with the shifting of his hips.

"Can you catch me?" he asks with a huge grin.

I grasp his hardon like a vice in my hand, and he groans. "Mmmm fuck."

"Fuck yes I can," I mutter as his hands finger into my hair. He pulls my hair into a ponytail and holds it, as I take his cockhead into my mouth. I flick my eyes up as a thank you to him. When our eyes meet, it stirs something in me, something I'm not sure I am ready to admit.

I suck his head hard, as I rub his shaft with my right hand, my left firmly holding his hip. I push him against the counter and travel him with my tongue along the ridge under his meaty packed head. I pump my mouth then drag my tongue up and down his shaft, ending with a hard suck of as much of his cock, as I can fit into my mouth. When I'm about to gag, I slip off. Never been my strong point.

He cups his hands under my armpits to get me to stand, his face sporting a satisfied grin, then he flips me into my spot against the counter and pushes the upper part of me down on the countertop. He teases his cock at my pussy lips and penetrates me from behind. We both groan out.

He thrusts into me slowly, then ramps up to fast and hard rams.

"Oh, fuck me. That feels so good. Fuck me. I want you to fuck me." I press my hands flat to the countertop for some resistance as he pounds away at me. The skin on my ass hurts with each pound, but the pleasure feelings win. I'm moaning wildly, climbing my orgasm climax again as he ejaculates inside me, then slows his pumping.

He rests his forehead on my back and plants kisses along my spine before standing up. "You are so luscious, Mom. That was such a good fuck. You need to let me do that again and again. We'll never tell. Dad doesn't need to know."

I spin around and look him straight in his eyes. "Right. Son." I smile and giggle. "Well, that was hot and fun." Love satisfying his kink, though it leaves a tiny bad taste in my mouth but I'll survive.

"No shit," he says with a huge grin. "More drinks. Maybe we could take a soak in the hot tub before we grill." He is already pouring us each a fresh glass of wine.

"I'm in. Naked. Right?" I raise an eyebrow at him. I resist the urge to dab napkins on myself to wipe my pussy dry. Gazing into his eyes, I say, "I like your cum draining down my thighs."

"Mmmm. And with your cum mixed in, that's the only way." He raises an eyebrow. "Of course, naked in the pool," he says picking up both glasses and heading toward the sliding door out to the hot tub. "If you put a suit on, I'll just immediately take it off of you, so don't bother."

I chuckle. "Oh, I have like zero doubts about that. I'll get the towels and meet you out there," I call as I scamper to the master bathroom.

Chapter Four
BEND ME OVER

I pull out two towels and check my phone for messages while leaning on the counter. I have a call from a friend and an unknown number. I roll my eyes. "I'll check you all later." I tap my phone closed. Running a washcloth over my genitals, I smile at myself in the mirror, slip my dress over my head, then smooth my tousled freshly-fucked hairdo. Sebastian is such a giving lover for a younger man. "Damn. You are lucky, Ru." I want to voice out loud that he's a keeper, but that statement is too young to live in the air of the world just yet. If ever, it can. Plus, he might not even want that. I shrug and spin around. No time like the present for this fantasy to further unfurl.

As I walk through the cabin, our words exchanged over text play through my head. How I seriously thought he was joking when he first wanted to hook up with me. Why would a man so young be into me? I had that thought almost daily when we first texted until finally, it sank into my head that this man really wanted me. The real me. Me! And if I'm honest, being twenty years older than him, it took me a little bit of time to think of him as a man, but, clearly, he's a man. Boy, am I so fucking glad I caved to his persistent requests. I know MILF is a phenomenon, but, still, it was shocking and still is, but I'm gonna love the shit out of this, whatever it is for as long as it lasts. I press a finger to my lips to shush my inner doubts. Just remember to savor, Ru, a phrase that came to me once when I woke from a deep sleep. It was as if someone had whispered it into my ear.

I open the sliding door and he has already removed the cover and is soaking in the hot tub. Pylons of steam obscure his face, making it more visible and less as it rises in waves. I take a step onto the cold deck boards and shiver as a chilly wind gust thrashes my naked body.

"Brrr," I squeal. I drop the towels on the table and scramble into the steaming hot tub as fast as I can.

He passes me a full wine glass, his face ever showcasing that amazing smile of his, as I sink into the heated water.

"Ah, this is delicious. Feels so good." I release a gratifying sigh.

"Indeed. It feels amazing." He sips wine, and a satisfied look nestles across his face as he sighs. "See. I knew we'd be compatible. You were so doubtful."

"Well, yes I was. And you know why. We talked about that." I stare at the waterspout spilling water out of the jet on the other side of the tub, it bubbles up as a dome at the top of the water. I know his statement is supposed to make me feel better, only it serves to make me feel more awkward.

"No need to revisit. Just know that I'm loving being here with you and fucking your brains out." He gives me a naughty grin. "What's next?"

I settle into the backrest as the jet pummels my back. "Um. Hot tub relaxing. Then when you are recharged, we still have the office and the spare room to grace with our sexual prowess. But ... we might want to eat first. Need food to fuck. Plus, there's tomorrow. But I'm game whenever you are, just remember we have all day tomorrow too." I know I said that twice but focusing on the positive. And then ...

"True. We have time, and we've already done so much." He leans over to kiss me on the forehead. "And for dinner, I'm going to be the grillmaster, so if you want to do your salad and potato stuff inside, that will work out. Divide and conquer." He secures my arm in his hand to pull me close, so I lean my head back on his shoulder.

"Perfect. Geez. This is just perfect. It's gorgeous here, isn't it?" I sigh and scan the scenery of the mountains and tree-packed slopes, snow already topping the peaks. "I think I could live here too."

"Yeah?" he asks dreamily. "It is certainly beautiful." He dips the stem of his wine glass into the water, swirling it around. "It smells really nice out here too. Might be the autumn smell or the pine trees, but it just smells … I don't know. Good."

"Fresh. I think it smells fresh."

"Yeah, good word for it." He nods. "You know, I don't need kids. I just need you."

I drop my eyes to the water swirling, to the bubbles popping, forming, dissipating. I can only nod and briefly meet his gaze. He pulls me close and thankfully he drops it because the lump in my throat is about to edge me to tears.

We finish our wine, French kiss for a few minutes, savoring each other's wine-soaked lips, warmth, and closeness.

"Let me get out first and get your towel ready. I'll hold it open, and you can run into it." He rises out of the water, and with lusty eyes I watch his sexy body move. "Let me take care of you, Ruan."

"Thank you," I say. "You pamper me. I like it." This man is a true gem. And a gentleman, so considerate of me always.

I watch him shiver, as he dries off and wraps the large fluffy towel around himself. It's way too small for him in this frigid air, even though it's large, most of his skin is still exposed. He holds open my towel and nods.

"Okay. Ready? Go!"

I rise out of the water and gasp, as the brisk wind brutally lashes my skin making it feel brittle. "Oh, fuck that's so cold!" I squeal, rushing into the towel.

He wraps me up and bear hugs me, curving his head and shoulders around me like a shelter. I just melt right in to him.

We shuffle huddled together into the cabin. The heat inside blasts us immediately, yet I still shiver.

"So hot then so cold and now warm." I shudder again. "Okay. Damn." After my shiver ends, I say, "Let's get dressed and cook. I'd cook naked but I'm too cold right now."

"Mmmm. Maybe we can cook breakfast naked." He nods with pursed lips, his eyes churning with hidden ideas.

I nod back. "Good plan." I give him a little smile and a cock of my head. "Would love to see those man buns of yours in front of the frying pan in the morning."

He raises an eyebrow and grins. "You got it, babe."

Once dressed and back in the kitchen, I start on the potatoes. I flip my phone on to some easy listening music, as I watch him out on the patio uncovering the grill. This feels so normal. Whatever that means.

I pull out the bag of mini potatoes from the fridge and wash them. Humming while I work drying the potatoes, I spin around and jump because he's a foot away from me. "Oh, shit! You scared me."

He wraps his arms around me. "I've just been enjoying watching you. I've dreamt of this very moment so many times. And here we are. Finally."

I snuggle my head against his chest as my arms wrap around him.

His cock is a rock against my gut, and I giggle. "You are hard again? I love it."

"You make me hard." He drops his lips to the top of my head. "I can't help it. You are so fucking sexy. I just want to ram myself into you again. Make you come on my cock."

I snicker. "Quickie? Then I need to get these potatoes in the oven." I glance back at the potatoes as he scoops me up in his arms.

"Oh, I have no problems doing a quickie. I can be real quick when I want to be. Never a problem."

He curls me to his chest and runs with me to the office, I'm giggling so hard as he grunts running. I imagine we must look like cartoon characters.

Mmmmm. Wow. Even him running while carrying me feels like foreplay.

Setting me down in front of the large dark wood desk, covered in only a lamp, a mug of pens, and a mousepad, he gives me a deep French kiss. He presses his body against me, and the edge of the desk pokes its ridge into my ass cheeks.

My pussy is throbbing, as he rubs my dress up then fingers me.

"Mmmmm. So wet so soon," he murmurs as he kisses my neck.

"You do that to me," I whisper, leaning back against his arm supporting, steadying my shoulders.

He grabs my hips and slides me on top of the desk. Teasing his hard cockhead against my pussy lips, he penetrates me.

We both groan out as if it's the first time we've fucked. He pumps into me for a short time, then grabbing my hips, he slides out of me and flips me around so fast I barely have time to take a breath. He pushes me forward onto the desk. My breasts, still covered in my dress, smash into the hard surface, and my hands smack the wood.

He growls, enters my pussy, and rams himself into me as I moan.

"Oh, fuck yes, Sebastian. Fuck me. Oh, fuck yes. Fuck me. I want you to fuck me," I chant, as he thrusts into me. I'm moaning like crazy.

He grabs my right arm and bends it, pressing it to my lower back, as he pounds into me ferociously on repeat.

This makes my breasts move more upward and wildly swing, as I lift myself off the desk slightly. This is better, my tits are probably more visible to his eyes this way as they gyrate past the large armholes of my dress.

The hard slams reverberate through my clit, and his cock rubs my G spot so aggressively, I'm almost close to coming with even just a quickie, the benefits of multiple rounds of fucking in one day. This man has got mad fucking skills. Now that's talent! Fuck me!

"Yes. Yes. Yes. Yes. Please. More. Yes." I lift my head, and he grasps my hair, pulling my head back, each nerve ending at the end of every strand of hair screams out to me sensually. I fight but lose as my head tips back further. He's got me.

"You are mine," he says in a pussy-wetting commanding tone.

He pounds me so fast and hard I slam into my orgasm, and to my surprise, I come as my body gyrates on the desk. As my pussy squeeze-grips his cock, extra wetness floods my pussy, and I sense his hard-on shrinking.

We are both panting hard as he lays his head on my back. "Office officially christened," he says in a breathy voice. "Fuck. You just turn me into an animal. I didn't hurt you, did I?"

"No. You did not. In fact, you made me come really hard."

"Ha! Knew it. I know right when it happened too," he says. "I noticed the clenching, and I'm learning how your body moves when you come." He lets out a long low sigh. "Fuck that felt good. I love the way your pussy milks my cock when you orgasm. I literally can't keep my cum in me when you do it."

"I rather like you losing control. It's hot as fuck."

He stands, and I straighten my body and spin around. "Yeah?"

"Hell yeah."

We share a peck on the lips through our smiles.

He grabs my hand, and we walk toward the kitchen.

I smirk. "Good thing I fuck myself with toys all the time so I can handle this much sex." I shrug. "Though if I get sore, it will be worth it."

He stops walking. "Yeah, but I don't want that. I want you to enjoy. Maybe we cool it and save the rest for tomorrow."

I nod, as I pull him forward to walk again. "Maybe. We shall see. We can always do other things if the mood strikes."

"True. Now. Put me to work. Tell me what to do, my sexy chef."

We work together preparing our meal, him prepping the potatoes coating them in olive oil and seasonings while I work on the salad.

He takes the steaks outside to grill as I finish up in the kitchen, a very satisfied and goofy grin on his face as he strides out into the cold wind using his backside to greet the outdoors first. He yells out, "Ah! Brisk out here," as he ventures out jacketless into the cold.

"Good luck in that wind," I call then mutter, "I hope it doesn't kill our grilling plans."

I sip wine and lounge on the couch as I wait for the timer to go off and for him to join me.

When the food is done, we nestle into the puffy comfy couch to enjoy our meal in front of the flickering flames of the fireplace and those of a giant three-wicked candle on the coffee table. After enjoying brownies with wine, we mosey off to bed early.

Once in bed, we kiss and fondle each other, nuzzling, snuggling, touching, caressing.

"I want to fuck you again, but I'm going to hold off, so you don't end up sore. We have tomorrow to enjoy, and soreness shouldn't be a part of it." He runs his fingers through my hair. It's so sensual, and I love it, but it's also making me very sleepy.

I stick my lip out in a pout. "I bet I'd be fine. Really, I would be. Let's fuck."

"We don't need to. I want that pussy of yours enjoying every thrust, not cringing it. We wait." He lifts my chin, so our gazes meet. "Okay?"

"Deal." I give him a small smile. How does he have more restraint than I do? I suppress my chuckle as he caresses my hair, twirling a curl around his finger, then letting it unfurl.

We kiss again and snuggle into a spoon. He laces his hand through mine, and I pull our entwined hands to my chest, hugging our handholding to my happy heart.

"Good thing I'm exhausted. I think I'll crash fast, I don't know about you. I'm full and satisfied. Sexually and from food. It's been an amazing day, Ruan."

Even though his semi-hard cock is pressing into my back and he's ready to fuck, and really all I want to do is turn and play with it, I sigh and say, "Good night, Sebastian. I loved our fuck fest day."

"Me too."

"Sweet sexy dreams," I say, snuggling against his arm that is cradling my breasts.

"If they are about you and me, they are." He sighs happily.

I relish his hot breath as it bathes my neck and upper back.

I will miss that most of all. That's what I will remember on nights alone with my toys, and him making me come hard on repeat, loving me up, and his obvious feelings of caring for me, pampering me. I sigh with a smile as my eyes fall closed, feeling loved without him having said it.

Chapter Five
AMATEUR PORN STARS

The light wakes me in the morning. As I glance over at him, his eyes are closed and his breathing is slow and even. I slip out of the bed and cover my bare skin in my terry cloth robe. The sunshine streaming into the cabin gives everything an orange-yellow glow, just like the past few mornings. It's utter perfection. I want to sit with that glow with a coffee mug in my hand, and him by my side, my laptop beside me.

I set up the mug with mountains on it with the right amount of creamer and choose a dark roast. I push the button, and the rich deep aroma soaks so wonderfully into my nostrils. I breathe deep and sigh. I'll set up the tripod in the spare room so it's ready when he wakes with that raging hardon ... which just makes me giddy with anticipation. Relationships aren't supposed to just be about sex, but this weekend, that's all I'm asking for. I smile huge as I glance towards the spare room, my mind spinning for how I'll get it all set up for our homemade porn session. Who needs wedding rings when there's homemade porn to make! I chuckle silently, not me.

I leave my coffee to brew and grab my tripod setup from the counter. I hustle to the spare bedroom. Assessing the room, the dresser is the best platform for videoing. I assemble the tripod and slip my phone in and aim it at the bed. Laying down, I click the little remote to start recording. He's gonna wake up hot. I need this all set to go.

I scamper to my phone and watch the recording. I adjust the aim down a bit more and re-record myself. Tapping the video on, I smile as

I watch myself writhe on the bed. Perfect, I can get the whole bed in the frame.

In the kitchen, I find my coffee is done brewing. After splashing in a bit more creamer, I settle in the sunshine spilling across the couch. First sip is always ... ahhhh.

Before I get half done with my mug of coffee, he calls out from the room, "Where's my sexy baby?"

"I'm out here," I respond. "Drinking coffee." I know what his next words will be. My heart rate speeds up.

"I have the world's hardest morning wood ready for you. Wanna fuck?" His voice sounds husky with sleep.

I chuckle salaciously. "Yes, of course," I call back. "I have the tripod set up in the spare bedroom. Want to record our homemade porn this round?"

Instantly he appears in the door frame, like a damn superhero so fast, his hair all disheveled like proper bed head while a massive grin has taken over his face. "Oh? You do, do you? I'm ready." He sways his hips so his cock floats back and forth in the air in front of him. "Ready to become undone and spew your cum again, my sexy babe?"

Fuck does he look delicious, like a scrumptious dream standing there with that face, those lusty eyes, and that hardon shaking at me like a beacon. "With that raging boner, how could I possibly say no?" I take another pull of my coffee and carry the mug to the island. I grab a mint out of the little bowl and pop it in my mouth. "Coffee breath," I say as he approaches me.

"I like your breath anyway it is." He swipes a mint too and rubs my buns through my robe. "Sore ass today?"

"I'm okay." I smirk. "You, beastly wild spanker you." Well, I may be a little tender, but shhh!

"Yeah. I don't know that I've ever gotten quite that carried away with spanking like that before. You bring out the beast in me I guess."

I chortle at his use of "beast." We are on the same wavelength once again.

"Apparently and I'm all good with it all." I wave my hand in the air. "So. Let's go fuck, oh porn star, sir."

"We need porn star names," he suggests.

"Indeed. I mean, for you, Italian Stallion fits."

He sniggers. "Nice one." He strokes his cock. "And for you, Kreemy Goddess. Spelled K r e e m y."

"Love it! And I'm ready to spill cream on you."

"Yes. I seem to be in deep need to go into you deep, like a stallion in heat." He swings his cock at me, and I grab it. He flinches. "Oh, fuck yes. I need a cowgirl."

"Yippe kiyay." I swing my hand in the air in a circle, then drop my robe.

"Oh, nice ass. You wrangle many stallions with that hand?"

"Just aiming at you, my Italian Stallion of a cowboy." I sashay into the spare bedroom with huge swings of my hips, snap my fingers, and throw my arm pointing forward into the room. "Pronto, Toro. I need a bull."

"Oh, yes ma'am."

I grab the little remote. While pointing to the bed, I say, "Make me a saddle my pussy can cling to, will ya?"

He grins and scrambles to lay on the bed, cock obediently tick-tocking in the air.

I press the button on the remote to start recording. "Good boy." I crawl onto the bed and straddle his chest, pressing my bare wet pussy against his skin. I lean down and scoot back so I can kiss his mouth, his hands fly up to cup my breasts, then he slides them down to grip and fondle the curves of my hips.

My lust rages. I twerk my ass up for the benefit of the camera, well for the later benefit of us while watching, and squat above his cock.

"Oh, fuck yes," he says, as I grab his cock and line it up with my pussy lips. "Ride me like the wind, bitch."

"My pleasure, ya bastard stallion."

He grips my hips hard and I slap his hands away.

He laughs. "Oh, it's like that now. Okay. I'm all in."

I sit on his thighs in front of his cock with my back to him, so his shaft makes a line up my lower back. I lean forward and raise my hips up and down to stroke his cock with the crack of my ass cheeks.

"Oi," he says with deep appreciation. "Helluva nice move."

"Shut up and kiss me, cowboy." I swivel to face him and take his cheeks in my hands and smash my mouth on his.

His tongue immediately rides into my mouth with a groan, so I suck it, then slide my tongue along his. I take his lower lip in my mouth and suckle it, give it a nibble as I continue to gyrate my hips. I kiss his neck and make my way to his earlobe, which I heartily suck and then nibble before I bite down.

He yelps, flinches, which triggers his hands to find my nipples. He pinches both my nipples and pulls them out from my body.

I moan and arch my back, pushing my tits toward his face. "Oh, fuck yeah. Oh fuck. Clit twitch," I murmur.

"Mmmm, fuck yeah." He opens his mouth wide, and I almost squeal in anticipation as he makes my right nipple disappear into his mouth and much of my areola. He sucks me hard, pulling my nipple deep into his mouth to deepthroat it. Then he harasses my other nipple with his mouth as I moan.

I switch to sliding around on his belly, mashing my wet labia lips and clit against him, rubbing myself into a hot frenzy. "I need his cock in me, fuck!" I grab his cock and line it up with my slit, lightly I press myself down on the tip, then I slide really quick down his shaft because I'm so wet.

He moans, as I bounce on his cock. "Gawwwwwd, fuck!" he mumbles.

I gasp and moan too. "Mmmmm. Fuck that feels so good," I mutter breathlessly.

His hands fly to my hips, holding me as I ride his cock. Catching my gaze in an eye lock, he firmly holds my hips and thrusts up into me.

"Yes, yes, yes, yes, fuck yes," I chant as he pounds me from beneath.

His pelvis rocks back and forth slamming into me as he pushes my hips down. His thrusts slam my clit, the harder he pounds me, the closer I climb to my orgasm.

"Close," I whisper in a breathy voice.

"Mmmmm." He pile drives me from beneath in a mad frenzy.

Fuck. Such strength he possesses.

"Uh, uh, uh, yeah, yeah, yeah," I chant, squeezing his shoulders, digging my nails in. "Oh, fuck!" I dwell, savoring this moment. I'm about to come and I can't do anything to stop it. At the top of this roller coaster, joy, exhilaration are imminent, mixed with a bit of fear wondering how strong this crash and soar of an orgasm will last.

I shudder in anticipation. My vagina begins contracting as convulsions steal me. I fall forward, losing control of my body, as my torso gyrates forward in a failed attempt to curl. My limbs migrate toward my body, my mouth falls open, my lips purse, my toes curl up, as I slam into a series of contractions that squeeze his cock inside me. A gush squirts out of my pussy.

"Yes!" he exclaims. "You squirted!" He pounds me for a few more pumps, then while keeping himself inside me, he flips me to the bed into missionary, shifting us sideways to the video camera.

Smart man.

The shifting of position gives my sensitive clit just enough of a break.

"Side view now," he whispers. "We will love this move later," he says between pants.

My clit is literally screaming at me as he rage fucks me so fast I feel a second orgasm brewing. I gasp. Words are too hard. I whimper and grunt.

He belts out a low deep man growl that makes my clit lurch in my groin.

The familiar pressure near my belly button flares as he fucks me fast, hard, and deep. Endorphins are swirling in me like a heavenly storm, I can't keep my eyes open. Feeling sleepy, yet fully aroused, I pierce the silence with a scream, my eyelids tightly closed.

His arms, shoulders, tense further under my fingers, and he just savagely fucks me like an animal, slamming so fast I can barely manage to even swallow let alone think. The vision goes into flashes as if I might faint.

I peak, and my body twitches. Body shudders overtake me, as I lose all control, and my torso scrunches up, my neck curls my head toward my chest, and I can't keep my tongue in my mouth. Bursting through the climax my pussy squeezes him with multiple contractions.

He grunts three times, and the wetness inside my pussy blooms. His body relaxes as he slows his pumping down. With a sigh, he rolls his body and crashes on the bed next to me.

We are silent for about thirty seconds, then thirty seconds more.

"Holy fuck. That was unreal. Amazing. So good, oh, fuck was that so good." I turn to him, and our gazes meet. "Killer combo apparently with your morning wood and knowing we are being recorded."

He is panting so hard, but a grin breaks out across his face. "Raged the fuck out of me."

"Talk about 'I'm gonna fuck me like an animal,' holy fuck me, Batman!" I giggle and snuggle into the space between his arm and his torso. "I came so very hard. It was perfection."

He pulls me in so our bodies are flush, all skin to luscious speck of skin, every inch that we can possibly align touching. "I guess sleep gave me some energy. Wow. I like fucking raged."

"I know, right? And you made me cum, twice!"

"Yeah, I have a lesbian friend who always tells me that if a woman comes, try to push her through that sensitive period and go even harder and she will come even harder the second time." He runs his free hand down my hair, rounding down around my cheek, then securing my chin between his fingers, he lifts my face so our eyes can meet. "I guess it worked, huh?"

"Um, totally. No one has ever done that quite that way to me before. It was beyond amazing. You are a fucking rockstar porn star." I scoff. "I damn near fainted."

He chuckles. "Oh, damn. Well, I'm well versed in sex, being obsessed and all. Yeah, and we got all that on the recording too. Sweet! I can't wait to watch myself pound you into oblivion."

"Well, I definitely went somewhere just now, oblivion seems right, like a dream-like euphoria. Seriously, Sebastian, that was probably the strongest sexual high of my life." Might be sappy but I don't give a fuck.

He grins and squeezes me in a bear hug. "Music to my ears, my love. And I want to do it all over again. But if I don't eat something soon, I might start gnawing on this pillow."

There's that word again.

"Right. Let's eat." I roll toward the edge of the bed, searching for the remote. "We fucked the remote lost," I say with a giggle. I slide off the bed and lower down on my hands and knees and spot it under the bed. I reach for it as his hands grip my hips.

"Damn, that pose is raging my desire to fuck you again. But my stomach is growling something fierce." He breaks out into the Frank Sinatra song about pizza pie.

"I'd eat pizza for breakfast." I stand up and play with my lips with my tongue as I raise my eyebrow. "Maybe I don't cook naked, I'll cook in my robe so we can actually accomplish cooking and eating without breaking out into another fuck session."

"Good idea. I'll go get something on too because apparently, we can't control ourselves worth shit."

I tap the remote off button to stop recording. "Can't wait to watch that playback. And I'm beyond thrilled I got you singing on video too."

He snickers at me with a silly expression. "It's going to be killer hot."

I nod. He heads over to the master bedroom to get dressed and I make my way to the kitchen.

Chapter Six
NOT DONE YET

Omelets for breakfast with lots of veggies, cheese and ham, and frozen hash browns. The shower hums from the bedroom, and I bite my tongue and freeze. No, I need to resist the urge to charge in there and join because we need to eat, not fuck again. Well, maybe we need both. But I want to see that body of his all dripping wet again. I shake my head as I pull the peppers, mushrooms, onion, and tomato out of the fridge. "I'm a nympho," I mutter.

He appears in the kitchen after a few minutes, as I am finishing chopping the veggies into little pieces.

"A fuck and a shower. Now that felt amazing. Unbelievable really. Now, delicious food and you. I might be in heaven."

I nod. "Yep. Same. I'm having such a fabulous time with you. I'm bummed you have to leave today." That sentence weighs my heart down to my toes.

"I know. It sucks. But no one is stopping us from repeating this, right?" He leans on the island with both arms supporting him. "I'm game to plan our next already."

I smile. "True. Right. And, honestly, I'd really love to, if you are game." He will text me when he gets out of here that it's over.

"Oh, I'm more than game. I'm totally in. I'd love to meet you again. And again. And again."

The look on his face makes me believe him, mostly, and the twinkle there sets my tummy into a flurry. I wave my hand in the air. "Okay. It's a plan. Now, for breakfast, it's omelets and then I was thinking we haven't gone for a swim yet, so that might feel good." I grin sheepishly. "I turned up the thermostat this morning so it would be warm. And honestly, I just want to see your skin all wet and dripping again."

His mouth curls into a naughty grin. "Ditto. And. Perfect. Then maybe we can squeeze in one more romp before I have to leave for the airport." The lust in his eyes tickles my belly.

Despite my desire for him, my heart sinks at the mention again of him leaving. "Oh, how I adore your sex drive." I pour the veggies into the frying pan as I savor that look on his face. "Oh, I do hope we have time to, yes."

"We can do it. I've got my suitcase all ready. So, I don't have to do a thing but secure an Uber and walk out the door. We can fuck until I get the text."

"Love it." Would he stay longer if I asked? I squash the flicker of panic rising in my gut. I can't breathe.

He comes around the island and grabs a mug to make a cup of coffee with the Keurig, his face full of joy and hope.

I crack the eggs into a large bowl, add milk and scramble it aggressively with a fork. The nearness of his body is so comfortable.

"Not sure how often I can swing a plane ticket, but you are always welcome to come and visit me too in Florida." He stirs the creamer into his coffee and then raises his eyes to meet mine. "You know that, right?"

"True. I could do that sometime. No strings. Just sex. I get it." I nod.

He grins at me. "Let's just say let's have fun together."

"Agreed." I pour the milk and egg mixture into the hot frying pan, add veggies, ham, and cheese. "One mega omelet coming your way." I peek at the potato cakes in the oven. They have a long way to go before they are done.

"I can't wait." He settles at the island on the barstool. "You look like you have it covered but put me to work if there's something I can do to help."

"I'm good right now. You sit and enjoy your coffee."

"Oh, I will, and I enjoy watching you move even more. You really are so very beautiful, Ruan."

"Thank you." I almost blush, but grin at him instead before I flip the cooked egg over to seal up the omelet. "Almost ready. Do you like ketchup with your hash browns?" I switch the oven to broil to get the potato cakes to brown up quicker.

He gasps. "Is there any other way? I mean, hot sauce would be my second choice if ketchup isn't available, but I'm a ketchup-a-holic."

"Oh, me too. Love the stuff." I dig the ketchup bottle out of the fridge. When I straighten up, his hands massage my hips from behind and slip into the slit at the front of my robe.

"How's that pussy? She lonely?" His fingers quickly find my pink wet spot.

I moan, as his fingers play with my lower lips. "Yes, she is." I lean back against him with a groan, nestling my head into his chest. He is so fucking delicious.

He embraces me in a hug with both arms around me from behind and I sigh again. "Sorry, I couldn't resist taking a quick tickle of that lush pussy of yours." He releases me.

I shovel the omelet onto a plate. "Yeah, we don't want your omelet to burn." Scooping the hash brown quickly onto his plate, I pass it to him and point to the ketchup. "Take your pull of that stuff to your heart's desire. I can't take it with me on the plane so have at it." Love a man obsessed with my pussy.

"When do you fly home?" He squirts a huge dollop of ketchup onto his plate, which makes me smile.

"I'm here for the week. I'll do some writing on my latest book once you leave. Plus, I have some revisions I need to do on another. So, I will be quite busy."

"I wish I could stay longer but I've got work and no vacation time left at the moment." He frowns as he adds one more splat of ketchup to his plate.

I stifle my amusement. "I totally understand." But ...

"But I do want to do this again. Can we? Will you?"

"Absolutely I want that. Very much so." I take a deep breath. "I want your cock in me and your lips on mine, your hands on me, and your eyes holding my gaze." I busy myself with making my omelet as he takes a seat at the island. My heart flutters a warning. "And please enjoy, don't wait for me. I want you to eat it while it's hot. That's when it's the best."

"Are you sure? I'm totally fine waiting."

"Please don't wait. It actually adds stress to me so I'd rather you eat and enjoy than be sitting there starving waiting on me." I grab the bowl of veggies. "Besides, I'll be beside you in no time here."

He smirks. "I get that. I'd feel the same way. Thank you. I'm ravenous and this looks delicious." He lets out a long sigh. "You spoil me."

"Oh. I think you are the one doing the spoiling. And I love both your food appetite and your sexual appetite."

"Yeah, I'm a bit insatiable on both fronts," he says with a throaty chuckle.

I finish up my omelet and join him at the island. I grab for the salt and pepper and he's already holding them up for me. We eat and chat, our playful gazes meeting every so often. We clean up the kitchen, complete with rubs, pinches, caresses, and French kisses, prepping in flirty clothed foreplay for our final fuck of the weekend.

"Okay. A skinny dip in the pool, then a final fuck. Where shall we go for the last one? Or should we just make it spontaneous?" I ask. The word "final" almost gets stuck in my throat. I shake my head trying to shed the knot in my gut. Just enjoy, Ruan.

"Spontaneous works. We christened all the rooms, but, you know, we missed both bathrooms. We might need to take a cabin road trip with my cock in you to each of them to call the cabin fully christened."

I chuckle. "Good plan. I like it." I start to strip, which takes me only a second to drop my robe to the floor. "Then we can fuck on the fly and see where our bodies take us." I sprint toward the sliding door. "Last one in is a rotten egg!" I call back to him. I glance behind and now he is sprinting for the sliding door, gaining on me quick with those long legs. I squeal as I pull the door open and race toward the steaming pool.

He had way more clothes on than I did so he is still stripping at the sliding door while I sink into the warm water. "Damn that air is so cold. I'm so glad I took the time to uncover the pool while you finished up the dishes. And ha-ha, you are the rotten egg and I'm all warm and toasty."

"Oh, I'll get you my little pretty." He shuffles quickly over the cold concrete, wincing as he quickly skates toward the pool, the cold deflating his boner a bit.

"Don't slip!"

He ignores me and runs to the pool. Safely sinking into the water, his face relaxes as he sighs. "Ah yes. That's much better."

We both twirl about in the water, easily swimming the full length quickly since it's such a small pool.

"A perfect little pool. This is really all you need for enjoying it." I glide in the water. "Damn. It always feels so amazing to swim naked."

"You alone in this amazing cabin the rest of the week seems like such a waste. I should be here to fuck you during your writing breaks."

I laugh. "I probably would get a whole lot less done if you did." An abrupt look of sadness drifts across his face. "Oh, no! I didn't mean it that way. I would actually have loved it if you could have stayed all week and I'd love you distracting me and consuming all my time with sex. I'd really love more of all of you." My heart does a happy dance, cheesy as that is, I love it.

Thankfully, the look on his face calms into one of lust instead. "Oh, you have no idea how much I wish I could do that. I'd probably lose my job if I don't show up tomorrow though. They are already laying people off; one screw up and I'll be the next to go." He rolls his eyes.

"Yeah. Totally not worth it." I swim to the opposite edge of the pool, and he swims fast right at me.

He catches my arm and pulls me to him. "I'd much rather be here with you, though."

My large breasts crush into his chest, as he presses my body to his. I meet his open mouth and we fall into a deep kiss. I press my tummy to his boner with a groan, trapping it deliciously between our bodies. "Oh, fuck. You are so hard again." I reach down and grab his cock and stroke it in the warm water.

He grabs my ass hard, and I flinch. He sighs. "Oh, I'm sorry," he murmurs. "See. I did spank you too hard. Dammit. I was hoping to bend you over the pool edge and smack that wet ass." A naughty grin slides across his face.

My pussy flares, and my clit twitches. "You still can. I'll let you."

"Nah, I'm just gonna fuck you nasty raw instead."

"One last chance," I murmur, running my hand over his wet shoulders and down his muscular biceps. "You are so fucking sexy. I can't believe I get to fuck you."

He leans back. "See, now you can't believe you get to fuck me? What the hell? I'm the lucky one here. You are sexy as fuck. I've searched for the perfect cougar, the sexiest MILF, and I stumbled upon you. You are seriously my fantasy woman in all respects. And that erotic brain of yours. Fuck me stupid." He licks my lips and pokes his tongue onto mine. He whispers into my open mouth, "I'm the lucky one who gets to fuck you. You are a goddess. And don't you ever forget it."

Just the perfect thing to say.

We kiss as his hands press my back so our full fronts touch.

My nipples harden in the cool air, as he holds me up out of the water so he can suck me clear to my areolas.

His tongue rides the bumps and he snakes his tongue along the gathered skin that builds up to my erect nipple.

My lust urges me to give him everything, all of me. I want that.

"Mmm. I love your nipples. They are so hard." He dives his mouth to devour me, and I arch my back making my breasts peak for him in the brisk air.

His other hand massages my free breast. He smacks his mouth while pinching my nipple, then twisting it slightly with a pull at the end. "We've been so busy fucking we've forgotten to use all your sex toys."

I sigh. "Aw, shit. You're right. But it's been so good anyway. So good." I sigh deeply. "But you did use the paddle."

"Ah true. We aren't total failures in the toy department." He trails kisses across my cleavage to mouth molest my other nipple. "I can't get enough of you. I'm addicted."

I reach down and stroke his shaft, his cock at full hardness, the tip slightly purplish in the natural light. I gasp as panic grips me. "We haven't sixty-nined yet either. We need to do that before you go." Do not cry, squash it.

"Don't worry baby, we will when we go inside."

My panic settles as I moan, his hand drifting down through the water to play with my pussy erases my sadness, at least for now. I let my thighs fall open as he slips his fingers inside me.

He rapidly fingerfucks me, making the water swirl all around and into me. He kisses my neck and presses my clit with his thumb causing me to yell out a loud moan. "Had enough swimming yet?"

"Yes," I murmur. "I want you to fuck me. I want you in me now. I want as much of you in me as possible."

He tangles his hands into my hair as we kiss, my hair ends dipping into the water. "You want this cock?"

I moan dipping my head back, wetting my hair further. How I love his hands in my hair. "Yes," I whisper into his mouth. "Yes. I want it so bad."

He is fingerfucking me, making the water gush toward my genitals in a rush.

He is consuming me. And I'll feed him.

He pulls me to the pool stairs. As he rises out of the water, the steam rolls off his naked skin in rolling waves, the curves of his ass cheeks undulating, as he climbs the stairs.

I reach up and cup his right ass cheek in my palm. The cold air immediately makes me shiver. My breasts and nipples tighten even harder in the cold brisk air. I rise fully into the cold and shudder even though the sun is beaming down on us. Skipping the use of towels, we rush to get inside, barely getting the sliding door closed before we tangle ourselves into each other. We are so hungry for each other you'd think we hadn't fucked all weekend.

He walks us to the fireplace as one, me walking backward, him securely holding my back. He gently pushes me down in front of the fire, our wet skin glistening in the golden glow. He licks the water drops off my breasts and kneels beside me as I lay fully flat on the carpet.

Without words, he lays down beside me, his face even with my pussy. The wet dewiness of his skin is so sensual as he moves, his skin lusciously shining across the supple mounds of his muscles with each movement. His hair wetted in chunks to his scalp. He pulls me on top of him, his cock springing in my face. He grasps my thighs in that hungry way that wets me further, he crashes his mouth on my soaking pussy, his nose nestling between my ass cheeks.

I sigh, as I open my mouth and close my lips around his cockhead. I slide my mouth up and down while pressing my tongue to his hardness, feeling it up, caressing it. I moan as he once again takes my clit into his mouth, my moans quickly rage up to grunts. I gyrate in motion with him as he takes long tongue swipes of my pussy lips, then smashes his face fully into my crotch.

"My pussy. I'm gonna make you come again." His hot breath bathes my clit. His claiming ownership of my pussy makes my clit throb. He takes my clit into his mouth for a hard suck, and I fall off his cock in a torrent of moans.

We are writhing against each other's bodies as we both suck, full moist skin on skin, the warmth of the fireplace melting away the cold, drying off our pool water drips as we sixty-nine against the flicker of the fire. The only sounds in the cabin for a few moments are our slurps.

My wet hair clings to my skin and I'm wonderfully completely unobstructed by loose hair, I bounce my mouth on his hard cockhead, swivel my tongue all around his head and ride it down his hard shaft in several licks before consuming his head inside the seal of my lips again.

He flinches. Pushes me off his cock and rolls me off in one swift motion. "Ah, fuck. Let me just eat you, I need a break or I'm gonna come, and I don't want it to end yet."

I lay back and my lust envelopes me as does the heat blasting from the fireplace. "I want you all over me. You feel amazing."

"Mmm. As do you my sexy cumslut." He nuzzles his bristled face against my thigh followed by the travel of his tongue making a trail of wetness upwards. He whispers over my pussy, "Come for me, baby. Come for me. Okay? Please. I want to taste your sweet cum once more." He pounces on my pussy with his mouth, suctioning strongly to my loose skin making me gasp and moan, thrash and writhe with pleasure.

My heart races, as he craftily edges me along. I whimper, grabbing at my breasts as his mouth makes wet slurping sounds as he thoroughly soaks my pussy with his saliva.

"Yes. Oh, fuck yes." I scream out when he presses his tongue flat on my clit and rides it up and down without lifting his tongue off me. That constant firm pressure gets me, just like my wand. It's amazing to me how he's learned my sexual needs from afar, all those months of us playing over a long distance.

He presses his fingers into my vagina, reaching for my G spot as he aggressively sucks my bits of flesh into his mouth. My eyelids flutter as he brings me closer to the height of my climax. He comes off my skin to say, "Squirt my face, baby. Do it." He sighs and blows a breath on my clit. "Let me taste this sweetness again."

My hair falls now that it's drier, curls flailing onto the carpet, as I thrash my head back and forth while gripping the sides of his head.

His mouth roughs up my pussy, and I fling my arms to my sides and dig my fingers into the carpet. "Aw, my gawd, fuck. Uh. Ah. Oh, fuck." I moan like he is murdering me as I charge up the hill toward the peak of my climax. Soon I will come for him and grant his wish. I fall silent as I teeter over the edge, crashing off the top of my orgasm, my body curls, my head dips to my chest and convulsions spill out my pussy, radiating through my body causing it to gyrate, jerking up and back in waves of intense pleasure.

"Mmmm, yes. My good girl," he exclaims, licking me like a lollipop, then full-on sucks at my opening.

It's too much; I push on his head to get him off my clit, but we are solidly entwined, he is embracing me so securely with his arms around my thighs. Relentlessly he eats at my pussy as I squirm and scream.

"Uh, uh, uh," I whimper, as he mercilessly sucks my sensitive clit. "Fuck!"

He releases me and stands up.

The orgasm was so strong, I'm left feeling weak, floppy, mushy, yet with my clitoris throbbing, and I'm sleepy, so out of it. Since I don't move, he scoops me up and carries me. Weaving his way through the furniture in the living room like a quarterback, hugging me close and curling his head down to me while he scoots. He's carrying me like he's stealing me to devour me in the master bathroom.

Ah yes. Christen the bathroom before he leaves. So delightfully thorough he is.

"Can you stand yet?" he asks in a very kind voice once we are in the bathroom, in a voice that melts me to my core.

I nod, I think I can, albeit wearily.

He sets me down and presses me onto the counter. I shiver still unsteady. Laying my upper body on the cool marble countertop, grateful for the unmoving structure. My nipples harden, making the skin of my breasts shiny and taut.

My boobs rub forward on the counter as he penetrates my pussy from behind. I lay my hands flat on the countertop and watch his face in the mirror, as he thrusts into me, our gazes meeting periodically in the reflection. My belly hits the cabinet harshly as he into pounds me.

His eyes point downward as he watches his cock entering and leaving me over and over again. I wish for such a view. I smile; he's such a masterful lover.

The skin smacks echo in the bathroom as do our grunts and moans as we make love one last time. I go up on my tippy toes each time he thrusts into me.

He grunts and pulls out of me. Scooping me up once again, he cuddles me to his chest.

"I want to see your eyes in this last moment. Savor the look on your face as we fuck. Dare I say, make love."

I caress his chest before he lays me on the bed. I smile at him as I happily spread my legs, his words dancing deliciously in my brain.

He climbs up the bed and gives me a short deep kiss and kisses each nipple before lining up his cock at my pussy. As he pushes himself into me, I moan out, matching the deep satisfactory appreciation in his own moan.

Our eyes lock as he pounds into me. His generous gaze cradles my vulnerability before I lose sight of him as my eyes roll back.

"Look at me, baby," he gently commands. "I wanna see those beautiful eyes of yours. Honestly, they turn me on the most."

I gasp and focus my stare to align with his. My climb up the orgasm is a rapid jaunt as our intimacy thickens in our mutual gaze. I lose my grip quickly and again my body is ravaged, rocked, controlled by the will of my clit as I come on his hard thrusting cock, our eyes still locked.

I whimper-moan, as he grunts and thrusts faster. He spills inside me, coating my pussy as quickly his drained cock shrinks inside me.

"Oh, fuck," he mutters, as he slows his pumping and then stills.

He falls on me. The weight of him crushing me, but I'll take it because soon he will be gone. A wave of tears threatens to push out of my eyes, both surprising and shocking me. I bite hard on this emotion and swallow it down to the blackness hiding in my gut. With every speck of me, I want him to stay.

"That was unbelievable, Sebastian," I whisper, my clit throbbing out in aftershocks. "My clit says she's happy."

He rolls off of me and I can breathe again. He sighs before he says, "Good. That's how I want it. Yeah. So beyond amazing. Whew! Now that was a spectacular fuck. As if the others weren't, but geez—fuck! That was killer sex."

"I know, right?" I turn on my side and snuggle into him, resting my hand on his chest, my head on the crook of his shoulder. "Epic."

"Next time we do a blindfold. Feathers. Massage oil. Sex toys. Maybe explore something we've never done. And, ah shit!"

"What?" I ask, somewhat alarmed by the disappointed tone in his voice.

"We forgot to use the edible chocolate body paint!"

I laugh with relief. "Oh, shoot. We did forget that didn't we." I nestle further into his skin. "Next time." The sound of those two words thrills me more than I ever expected them to. Even if we only end up being fuck buddies, I'm thrilled with that. "I'm sure it will last. I'll check the expiration date. I can always buy more too."

I close my eyes as my skin savors the feel of his warmth.

"Yes. Well, hopefully, it won't be too long. We so need to hook up before it expires. I want my cock back in you already and I haven't even left this cabin yet."

I giggle and prop myself up on my elbows to look into his eyes. "I really had a lot of fun with you this weekend. Sebastian. Truly I did."

"You seem surprised."

I shrug. "No. I just didn't know."

He raises an eyebrow and pulls me back down to snuggle. "Well, I knew then, for the both of us."

He holds up his hand, fingers spread. I raise mine and match my fingertips up to his. My eyes drift from our touching fingertips to his eyes. We hold each other's gaze for several minutes, our fingertips resting upon each other. A shift clicks in my heart, and I wonder how this is possible that we have this connection that started just over mere airwaves. We were just an idea, a phone call, a text, and now we are this couple touching fingers in a rustic cabin in the middle of nowhere, but yet, I feel him everywhere in me. And I don't want him to go.

"No more doubts. I want you to know I loved every second of this weekend."

He smiles and finally speaks, "Me too. This was a dream come true for me. Being honest here. You've fulfilled so many fantasies for me. Next time I'm coming with a well-thought-out list of activities though." His grin is priceless.

I drop my head and laugh. "You'd better." My lust blooms at the mere thought of more sex with him, with new things with him, even if it's months away.

He glances at the clock and sighs. "I guess it's time for me to set up an Uber ride."

"Damn. That's a downer." Don't cry.

"Yep, definitely." He kisses me on the forehead. "But I've got no choice, babe."

"Yup. I know. I totally get it. Gotta eat. Gotta have a roof over your head."

"Indeed. And you see how much I eat!" He laughs, and I join him.

He rises from the bed to stand. "Better look for my clothes. I think I stripped and tossed them in my frenzy to get out the door to not be the rotten egg." He chuckles, as he's swiftly disappearing out of the bedroom doorway.

I pull myself out of bed and mosey to the door frame. I lean against the wood as I watch him search for his clothes and slowly dress. "I hate to see you get dressed," I tease.

"I know, right? But the Uber arrival time is short, only ten minutes, so I don't have much time." He slips on his socks and now his dressing is complete. He opens his arms. "Hug me quick in case he's early."

I run, and he encircles me in a big bear hug embrace.

"Until next time, my love," he whispers onto the top of my head.

"Until next time," I whisper into his chest. I lean back and gaze up into his warm brown eyes. "Soon."

He nods. "Soon."

His phone buzzes in his pocket. "Ah, see! I knew it! He's here already." He squeezes my naked body to his, then lifts my face to point directly at his, with both hands on my cheeks.

Tears threaten to spill, but I'm too strong for that. I'll wait until he goes.

"We aren't done," he murmurs. "Not even close."

We kiss deeply, even though there's a honk from outside.

I pull out of the kiss and reach up to caress his cheek. "Have a safe flight. Thank you for all the hot amazing sex. And the company." I smile biting my sadness back. "And yeah. We aren't done." A dam is about to burst in me, and I don't think I can stop it.

"And thank you. This has been one of the best weekends of my entire life."

I smile.

He smiles.

Being sappy together feels amazing.

We separate and I watch as he walks to his suitcase and grasps the handle firmly in his hand. "I know next time I won't need as many clothes."

I laugh. "Right? So true. Goodbye. Stay safe," I say, cradling myself with my arm under my breasts.

"Goodbye," he says as he turns toward me. "You stay safe too. And always think of me when you use those toys, eh?" He clears his throat. "Facetime me later. Please."

"Oh, have no doubt, I will." I shimmy my shoulders. "I might need to make you some videos in the meantime, huh?"

He grasps his heart and nods. "Please. Yes, please do. I'd love that so much. More and more of you. That's what I want." Then, with the last glimpse of his handsome grin, I wave as he pulls the door shut behind him.

I dash to the window and watch the car pull away. "It was good, lover. Be safe on your own. May we meet again someday and on this same wavelength we so wonderfully shared this weekend." My heart is both sinking and soaring at once. Feeling dizzy I need to sit down.

I locate my robe and slip it on. Dancing through the kitchen, I grab the remaining bottle of red wine we never even opened. Memories crash in on me and squash my tears as I smile. I refuse to tarnish this with actual crying. This weekend was too good for tears. Just not going to ruin it.

I stab the corkscrew in the cork. As I screw it in, I bite my lip and recall all our fucking and all the looks he gave me that sent chills down my spine, twitches through my clit, and butterflies around my gut. I pour a very full glass of wine and grab my laptop from the counter. I settle on the couch and open my laptop.

I say to myself, with a greedy grin, "And now, to write our story ..."

To be continued ...

RUAN'S GETAWAY SERIES CONTINUES WITH BOOK 2 …

I look into Sebastian's eyes through my phone. "I rented a beach house. It's on the ocean and just a short drive from your house."

"You did?" His face blooms with joy. "Where? When? Tomorrow?"

I laugh delighted with his response. "In five weeks. Can you swing time off?"

"I feel a sudden bout of the flu coming on." He chuckles, the tip of his cock bouncing into view.

"Perfect. I want you to fuck me on the beach, under the night sky blistering with stars."

"Just try and stop me, love. Every night for as long as you want."

"You are the best."

"I am my best with you."

ABOUT THE AUTHOR

Ruan Willow is an erotica author, sexuality podcaster, and erotic audiobook narrator. She is also published on Literotica and Lush Stories online. She loves interacting with fans, cooking, sex, reading, sex, being outdoors, spending time with family and friends, travel, swimming, sex, podcasting, and more sex. Did you catch all the sex? She's giggling right now thinking about you reading all about sex. Yup, she loves to laugh!

Thank you for purchasing this book! Pink Infinity Publishing LLC and Ruan Willow thank you!

From Ruan:

Thank you so much for reading my book! I happily wrote this in response to a fan's request. My fans are my main focus, but of course, I want to like what I write too, and I thoroughly enjoyed writing this story. I am where I am because fans responded to me and my writing so I owe everything to all of you. You are a blessing in my life, and you give me more joy than you will ever know. I love interacting with fans and I will never ever give that up.

This book is an erotic romance, heavy on the sex because that's what my fans love and I'm happy to oblige. I hope you read the upcoming books in this series as well.

If you'd like to experience more of my work, here is the link to my sexuality podcast, my books, my website, my Patreon, and my linktree with all my links.

Thank you for purchasing this book. I'd love to hear your thoughts in an honest review on the site where you purchased the book from. It warms my heart profusely when I see someone has taken the time to review my book. Love you all very much!

I want to thank all my family and friends for all of their support. I'd be lost without you.

Want Ruan to narrate your book? She has an account on ACX. Send her a message on ACX to get in contact with her.

Find Ruan and her podcast online:

All Ruan's Links in one spot on Linktree: https://linktr.ee/RuanWillow

Oh Fck Yeah with Ruan Willow Podcast: https://ohfckyeahwithruanwillow.buzzsprout.com/

Website is https://ruanwillowauthor.com/

Ruan's other books:
The Getaway Series:
Ruan's Beach Getaway. Book 2
Magic In Her Kisses
The Sex Challenge Series:
The Kitchen Sex Challenge Book 1
The Grocery Store Sex Challenge Book 2
Inside of Ruan Willow
The Mardi Gras Unmasking
Ruan is in the following anthologies:
He Will Obey
The Femdom Coven
Ruan is also a NSFW erotic audiobook narrator. Find her books for sale online.
Ruan also has stories on Frolicme dot com and Literotica.